# Praise for Frances Kazan

"Like an intricately patterned Turkish carpet, *Halide's Gift* is a complex tale of intrigue, secrets, superstitions and veiled passions set at the end of nineteenth century Constantinople, a time when change chafes against tradition and a place where East and West rub elbows. With a wealth of exotic detail resulting from meticulous research, Frances Kazan's sensuous writing draws us into the multi-layered life of a harem and two sisters whose different natures push against ancient proprieties, each in her own way, crystalizing the forces in turbulent conflict. She has turned unknown history into compelling human drama."
                                        — **Susan Vreeland, author of**
                                        ***Girl in Hyacinth Blue***

"We can't go back to Constantinople, but in this fictionalized biography Halide Edib teaches us much about women's lives in that eastern metropolis at the turn of the century...its portrayal of an Islamic world on the brink of change is carefully detailed and convincing."          **—*Publishers Weekly***

"Kazan has written a politically intriguing and uniquely stylized novel with a subject matter that is refreshingly untrodden. A master of Turkish studies, she conveys this story with the mystique of billowing incense."
                                        **—Elsa Gaztambide, *Booklist***

"A memorable read: heartfelt, historical, richly realistic."
                                        **—*Kirkus Reviews***

"Engrossing...Most of Halide's story takes place in the harem, where it engages themes of love, marriage and betrayal.... Kazan's descriptions of turn-of-the-century Constantinople are haunting."          **—*The Washington Post***

"A wonderfully foreign, fascinating world...[Halide] was a woman who defied convention." —*The Denver Post*

"This is an enchanting, engrossing novel. Frances Kazan has taken Halide Edib's true story—her amazing moment in Turkey's history—and with an alchemy of art and scholarship has turned it into the kind of fiction that illuminates a world." — **Jane Kramer**

"I was gripped by Frances Kazan's evocation of the last days of the Ottoman empire in *Halide's Gift*. That strange, fragile world of complex intrigues and compromises is made fully present through her scrupulous attention to individual lives and psychological truth. An impressive novel." — **Pankaj Mishra, author of** *The Romantics*

"*Halide's Gift* tells the story of a remarkable woman's life as it unfolds in the last years of the Ottoman Empire. The outer world of politics and society forms a wonderful counterpoint to the steady growth and maturation of this inspiring woman's inner life. Frances Kazan has given us in this radiant novel not only her rich insight into these incredible times, but also a new heroine whom we can admire and from whom there is so much to learn." — **Philip Glass**

"*Halide's Gift* will haunt you. The story is both moving and mysterious— the women passionate, complicated and noble. Frances Kazan is a writer of exceptional promise." — **Patricia Bosworth**

# The Dervish

# The Dervish

A NOVEL

FRANCES KAZAN

NEW YORK

ISBN: 978-1-62316-004-3

**Publisher's Cataloging-in-Publication**

Kazan, Frances.

The dervish : a novel / Frances Kazan. — New York : Opus, c2013.

    p. ; cm.

    ISBN: 978-1-62316-004-3 (print) ; 978-1-62316-005-0 (epub) ; 978-1-62316-006-7 (Kindle) ; 978-1-62316-007-4 (Adobe PDF)

    Summary: An American war widow seeks emotional asylum with her sister at the American Consulate in Constantinople during the Allied occupation in 1919. Through a cross-stitched pattern of synchronicity Kazan's heroine becomes a vital thread in the fate of Mustafa Kemal (later Ataturk) and his battle for his country's freedom. Based on firsthand accounts of the Turkish nationalist resistance, *The Dervish* details the extraordinary events that culminated in 1923 with the creation of the Republic of Turkey.—Publisher.

    1. World War, 1914-1918—Turkey—Fiction. 2. Turkey—History—Revolution, 1918-1923—Fiction. 3. Constantiople—History—Fiction. 4. Islam—Relations—Christianity—Fiction. 5. Atatürk, Kemal, 1881-1938—Fiction. 6. Mehmed VI, Sultan of the Turks, 1861-1926—Fiction. 7. Bristol, Mark L. (Mark Lambert), 1868-1939—Fiction. 8. Adivar, Halide Edib, 1885-1964—Fiction. 9. Adivar, Abdülhak Adnan, 1882-1955—Fiction. 10. Wilson, Woodrow, 1856-1924—Fiction. 11. Allen, Annie T., 1868-1922—Fiction. 12. Billings, Florence, 1879-1959—Fiction. 13. Dunn, Robert, 1877-1955—Fiction. 14. Historical fiction. I. Title.

PS3561.A933 D47 2013

813/.54—dc23 1302

A Division of Subtext Inc., **A Glenn Young Company**

44 Tower Hill Loop • Tuxedo Park, NY 10987

Publicity: E-mail OPUSBOOKSPR@aol.com

Rights enquiries: E-mail GY@opusbookpublishers.com

All other enquiries: www.opusbookpublishers.com

OPUS is distributed to the trade by The Hal Leonard Publishing Group

Toll Free Sales: 800-524-4425

www.halleonard.com

*For Joe and Charlotte*

I am warned by the dervish way—
You cannot become a dervish.
Come, if you wish, what can I say?
You cannot become a dervish.

**YUNUS EMRE**
*Translation, Talat Sait Halman*


*"Alum Yazisi"*
("Our fate is written on our forehead")
**OLD TURKISH SAYING**

# Prologue

NEW YORK, SEPTEMBER 1961

My colleagues have been urging me to write a memoir, Turkey is in the news again, a decade of democracy has come to a violent end, and the generals have seized power. A military coup dispensed with the government; the prime minister, Adnan Menderes, has been hung. Pictures of his crumpled body wrapped in a white garment like an operating robe have circulated among the opposition. A sign is slung around his neck as if he was a common criminal. Despite suffering this horrible death, his expression is peaceful. There had been a trial, of course. The prosecution presented accusations of betrayal and violation of the constitution, but the outcome was a foregone conclusion. Western governments protested the harsh sentence—even President Kennedy added his voice, but the generals are hard and insular men who care little for world opinion.

Writing a memoir was the last thing on my mind. The nature of memory is suspect, subject to change with the passing of time, but this death has stirred my anger. Menderes was decent man; this I know from friends who fought at his side during the Turkish War of Independence.

1

Now their dreams of democracy have once again been smashed by the tramp of army boots and the threat of a hangman's rope. I am rethinking my resistance to examining the past, but it's hard to know where to start.

I pull an album from the shelf and press the tips of my fingers against the label that reads "Istanbul, 1919," as if these words possess magical properties that can conjure up those early days. Memory can be a deceptive faculty. It's hard to say where stories begin and end. My arrival in Istanbul that distant, cold morning was preceded by years of pain and other stories with their own deep roots and wandering branches. The pendulum in the grandfather clock creaks back and forth. Time passes, relentless. I must get my story on paper, for time is running out.

I turn the pages of the album until I find the picture I am looking for, taken on the platform at Sirkeci Station moments after my arrival in Istanbul. There is my sister Connie, her arms curled around my waist, her embrace both warm and welcoming. It was late January, during the coldest, darkest winter in living memory. In spite of the icy wind that swept through the station like a malevolent spirit, the two of us are smiling at the cameraman, brought by Connie to commemorate the moment of our reunion. Above our shoulders you can just make out the words " ... des Grands Express Européens" written on the side of the train that brought me from Paris. Our eyes are wide from the flash, glistening with tears—or is that memory and perception playing tricks again?

We had not seen one another for five years; the Great War kept us apart. Connie's husband, John, was a diplomat. John was a gifted man, educated at Princeton, fluent in French and German. His restrained manner and balanced nature were well suited to his profession. He was a rising star. Despite my antipathy toward his privileged background and inherited wealth, Connie had made a good match; they adored one another. Soon after their marriage the State Department sent him to London, and three months later the assassination in Sarajevo sparked the Great War. Despite cruel fighting that devastated Europe, Connie's letters from London were cheerful, filled with details of consulate life, their elegant home, and lively parties. Following the signing of the peace treaty, John was dispatched to Istanbul, an unexpected posting—for him an important step on the career ladder, but for my sister a rude awakening to the reality of the life she had chosen. Istanbul was the dark heart of the Ottoman Empire, now ruined and demoralized after its ill-fated alignment with the German Kaiser. Connie wrote, begging me to join them. I agreed without hesitation. There was nothing to keep me in New York.

Almost eight weeks had passed since I set sail from the Brooklyn Navy Yard aboard an empty troopship bound for Calais on a mission to retrieve men who had survived the carnage. Storms drove us off course; huddled in my cabin, faint from the sway of the waves, I stared at the horizon waiting for the first sight of land. Safely on shore, I boarded the train bound for Paris, the center of the world in those chaotic postwar days. Soldiers, diplomats, and journalists crowded the wide boulevards, while day after day the Allied leaders sought a solution for world peace. I have no memory of how I passed my time until the military driver came to take me north to search for one lonely grave. Those early months of widowhood remain a blur. My loss was too profound to comprehend.

Even now, thirty years later, the scale of horror of the Great War astounds me. In four short years the confident, civilized nations of Europe had all but destroyed themselves. Governments shattered as the borders of Europe shifted and the vast colonial empires disappeared.

Imperial Russia lost more than a million men, only to be crushed by a homegrown revolution. Thousands of White Russians went into exile. The Austro-Hungarian Empire imploded, leaving a chasm in Central Europe. Kaiser Wilhelm, who was thought to be certifiably mad, fled to Holland, and Germany became a republic.

In 1913 the Ottoman Empire stretched from the Bulgarian border in Europe across the Anatolian plains into Syria, Trans-Jordan, Palestine, Mesopotamia, and Iraq. Yet only a handful of people in the Young Turk leadership supported the alliance with the Germans. Some blamed the influence of Enver Bey, one of the ruling triumvirate and a man infatuated with everything German. Others, including Henry Morgenthau, the former American ambassador, maintained that the Germans had plotted and schemed for years to infiltrate Istanbul and extend their Teutonic Empire across the Ottoman territories.

When the Ottomans finally surrendered at the end of October 1918, the minister of the navy signed an armistice composed and executed by an English admiral on board a battleship moored off the Greek Isles! This defective document made no provision for surrendering arms or munitions, an omission that would have far-reaching consequences. The Muslim army disbanded; demoralized and defeated, the troops straggled home to land ravaged by years of famine and war. Flouting promises made to the Ottoman government, the Allied victors sent a million soldiers to occupy Palestine and Mesopotamia and the major Turkish seaports. Despite protests from the sultan's government, the Allies sailed through the Dardanelles into the Marmara Sea and disembarked along the Bosphorus. Thousands of foreign troops poured into the ancient ports of the Golden Horn and took over the capital. Mehmed VI, caliph of all Islam, relinquished his power to the European commissioners, who divided the city into zones and set about maintaining order.

A few days before my arrival in Istanbul, General D'Esperey, commander of the French forces, landed at Galata. Mounted on a white horse, he rode through streets of the European quarter cheered by crowds of jubilant Greeks. It was a mocking gesture echoing the triumphant arrival of Sultan Mehmet II, otherwise known as Fatih the Conqueror, almost five hundred years before, when the Ottoman army sacked the last outpost of Byzantium and proclaimed Istanbul the new capital of the Islamic Empire.

The Germans were not the only ones casting a possessive eye across the lands of the Near East. During the Great War no less than three secret treaties were drawn up by the Allies, distributing the former Ottoman territories among themselves as part of the spoils of war. When the Paris Peace Conference convened, these secret deals lingered on the minds of the Allied leaders; no one knows for sure if President Wilson was aware of their existence. In his twelve-point plan for peace, the last paragraph declared, "The Turkish portions of the Ottoman Empire should be assured of secure sovereignty...."

All this I learned later. When I arrived in Istanbul that cold windy morning, I knew nothing.

# Part One

# 1

JANUARY 1919

Pale-faced soldiers lounged against the barrier smoking cigarettes, their half-closed eyes follow us as we hurried into the station yard. French, or were they English? I could not tell; their bland expressions gave no clue.

"Thank God you are here," said Connie, clutching my arm as if fearful fate might tear us apart again. "You're so thin and pale. We'll take care of you—bring you back to your old self."

"That old Mary is gone, Connie—don't look for her in me anymore. She no longer exists."

"It's early days yet. You will prevail—you were always the strong one."

"Two years."

"Two years is nothing. The loss you suffered was immense."

A pair of donkeys pushed between us, their skeletal frames bent by baskets crammed with stones. Connie was forced to let go of my arm as the poor beasts lumbered by and were soon swallowed up in the crowd. It was late afternoon and the station square was swarming with

9

people— men in starched collars and crumpled suits, on their heads windblown turbans or dusty red fezzes and women billowing in black or huddled in shawls, their eyes cast downward.

"Stay close, Mary, stay close. There are pickpockets and thieves on every corner."

"What of my bags?" Alarmed, I glanced behind to see that the crowd had closed in, trapping us in a sea of bodies.

"Don't worry, I paid the porters handsomely; they will guard those bags with their lives. So different from London—there the people had a code of honor even in the most difficult days of the war," she said wistfully.

I glanced at her out of the corner of my eye and caught an unguarded moment. There was a downward curve to her mouth, and a dark tinge to the half moon curve beneath her eye marred her rounded beauty. My sister seemed troubled. I hoped it was nothing more than the effects of the move.

"Seems we both have adjustments to make."

"I was looking forward to returning to New York, but John was so excited by this posting, what could I say? Istanbul is at the crossroads. What happens here will determine the future of this region."

A car was idling at the far end of the square, shades covering the windows; when we drew close a uniformed chauffeur rushed from the driver's seat to open the door. Connie slipped into the back seat. I hesitated, taking a last look at the teeming crowds.

From nowhere came an eerie wail. Moments later another cry echoed across the water and still another this time from the hill above the station; soon the air was filled with this strange cacophony made worse by the howling of dogs.

"The call to prayer," said Connie, patting the seat beside her.

"But it's late afternoon."

"Five times a day, seven days a week; we don't need a clock."

"What are they saying?"

"Allah is God, God is great." Connie beckoned, waving her hand with urgent energy. "Hurry, Mary, we have to leave. The curfew starts at dusk; even diplomats have to obey."

The American Consulate was housed in the Palazzo Corpi, an Italianate palace cloistered behind a high wall in one of the back streets of Beyoglu. A guard waved us through the gates, and as we crunched into the drive I saw John waiting at the top of the steps. He bounded toward the car, looking vigorous and sensual. Seeing him again gave me a sense of assurance. I was with family and safe, for now. As his arms folded around me, sadness gripped my throat like a chokehold. It seemed an eternity since a man had held me close.

"Thank God you are safe. We were worried. How brave of you to venture so far alone."

"I'm no fragile rose." I forced a smile.

"Don't make light of it, Mary. It can be very dangerous for a woman to travel alone through war-torn Europe. I had a lot of concerns."

"I could not stay in New York," I murmured, staring up at the arched and pillared façade. "Quite a building. I imagined a place more Oriental and exotic."

"There is exotic, a lot of exotic," said John, breaking into a smile. "You'll see in time."

"We have one of the best apartments; it's on third floor at the back facing the old city. The view is spectacular," said Connie.

"I wouldn't say that too loudly, darling," John said, guiding me up the steps with a touch on my elbow. "How long did you linger in Paris?"

"A couple of days."

"Car picked you up?"

"Did I thank you? I don't remember."

"No need for thanks, Mary. You are my sister. How else would you have found...," he hesitated.

"His grave?" I interjected.

"It's hard to imagine a man so in love with life dead and buried."

"If it hadn't been for that military driver and his guide I'd still be there," I said quietly. "There are so many graves."

"And northern France—how was it?"

"Rubble, burned out trees and villages—like a nightmare." I paused at the top of the steps, my heart pounding.

"Nature will take care of the destruction," said John. "Eventually the trees and bushes will grow back, fields will bear crops, villages will be rebuilt. It is our responsibility to find a way to live peacefully and ascertain nothing of this magnitude happens again."

We entered the palazzo through tall doors polished to a high sheen. John ushered me into an elegant hallway crammed from floor to ceiling with boxes, files, and oversized trunks stamped with the official seal of the United States Navy.

"It's not usually this chaotic," he explained. "Our new area commander, Admiral Bristol, moved into the consulate a couple of days ago."

"No one expected him to actually take up residence; we thought he was going to remain on his ship," said Connie, removing a dead leaf from one of the plants pushed out of place by a steamer trunk.

"Connie has prepared your room herself," said John, "and we have ordered a special breakfast to welcome you."

For the first time in months I felt suffused with affection. I had done the right thing coming this far.

The long hall was lined with glass-paneled doors etched with flowers; overhead the ceiling was improbably painted with cherubs and garlands of flowers in a style reminiscent of Fragonard. I looked at the reflection of my face in a mirror; a stranger stared back at me. Weeks of travel had thinned my cheeks, my eyes were creased with faint lines, and strands of unruly hair escaped from beneath my hat.

"This mansion was built by an Italian ship owner for his mistress," said Connie.

"Just a rumor," said John.

"You hate to admit this serious diplomatic edifice was once a monument to illicit love."

John moved on down the hall, weaving between piles of boxes, and then paused at an open door. "Why, Lewis, I didn't expect to find you here today."

"My offices are the best in the building; I don't want Bristol assuming he has the right to occupy them, so I am guarding my territory." The speaker had a tremulous voice, almost childlike.

"Allow me to introduce my sister-in-law, Mary Di Benedetti," said John.

"Lewis Heck at your service ma'am. Please forgive me for not getting up." The speaker was a man of indeterminate age who was lying on a chaise, his legs covered with blankets.

"Mr. Heck is our acting commissioner," said John.

"Do not be deceived by that weighty title," said Heck with a chuckle." I was here before the war with Ambassador Morgenthau. I am one of the few people who speak Turkish, so the State Department sent me back with a promotion."

"Your language skills are invaluable," said John.

"No one speaks Turkish except the ordinary people," said Heck. "I am good for buying flour and sending endless reports to our commissioners in Paris."

"Mary just arrived this morning, on the train from Paris."

"Paris!" echoed Heck. "I heard our president was riding about the city in an open carriage acknowledging the crowds as if he were royalty."

"I was only there for a couple of days."

"People are desperate for a resolution. They imagine President Wilson's plan will save the world, so they clamor to see him like they would a messiah."

"We must be optimistic, Heck; sooner or later the Europeans will understand Wilson is right. Self-determination is the only way. Colonialism is a thing of the past."

"You are indeed the man of the future," said Heck.

While they were talking, Connie wandered over to the window. She pressed her long fingers against the glass and looked out.

"There are sailors at the gate, John, quite a number. They are arguing with the guards."

"Sailors? Are they French, Italian?"

"American," said Connie. "The gates are opening. They're in the drive with a load of crates and what looks like a desk."

"Bristol's men, from his brig *Scorpion*," said Heck, closing his eyes. "The admiral will be with us any minute."

That first night it was impossible to sleep; I lay awake listening to the ceaseless barking of street dogs. Close to midnight I thought I heard gunshots. Alarmed, I sat up, wondering if it had been my imagination. Perching on the edge of my bed, I stared across the rooftops. Everything was dark save for a few flickering points of amber. The moon, on the cusp, cast jagged silver shadows across the sky. My painter's eye took over. To distract myself from thinking about Burnham, at an hour when the past was best left to dreams, I tried to imagine how I would capture the varying shades of black and gray.

Somewhere in my baggage there were sketchbooks, charcoal, and watercolor paints.

A door slammed. I heard footsteps and assumed it was John returning from his office. Moments later raised voices came from the direction of John and Connie's apartment. Feeling like an eavesdropper, I tried to ignore them, but the argument continued. Eventually it stopped. Silence fell over the household and I subsided into a restless sleep.

# 2

The first time I saw the old city was a few days after my arrival; John arranged an excursion on a morning when the consulate was closed. Before we left Connie wrapped herself in a shawl and tied a scarf around the lower half of her face. She insisted that I take the same precautions. A bitter wind had cleared the air of smog, and I was thankful for the extra layers. John brought his interpreter, Mr. Stathis, an elderly Greek who wasted no time telling me that he was fluent in all five languages spoken in the city at that time. The so-called upper class and educated elite were fluent in French; the Ottoman government even conducted business in French rather than their native Turkish. For as long as anyone could remember the Greek and Armenian Stamboulus had spoken their native tongue at home and Turkish in the street. Signs were written in three languages, and even the humblest porter had a grasp of pidgin French.

As we crossed the Galata Bridge my eye was drawn to the haze hovering over the rooftops on the hills ahead. It tempered the clarity of the white blue sky and cast a glow across the old city. Shading my eyes against the sun, I watched the gulls soaring through the minarets. Suddenly my view was obscured by cloud of smoke drifting across the windscreen, and the sound of a ship's horn shook the windows as a vessel passed beneath the bridge. We drove into an open square where a line of trams idled beside the quay. Fishing craft and rowboats were anchored close to the harbor wall; farther out the deeper waters of the Golden Horn were clogged with battleships flying Allied flags. They towered above the smaller craft, casting long shadows across the water.

We left the crowded square and climbed through a web of narrow lanes, on and on deep into the old city. The streets were crowded with men in the fez and turban and others wearing fur hats with flaps over the ears. The women were veiled or shrouded in heavy scarves, an illustration of travelers' tales come to life. We drove past dilapidated wooden homes crowded against one another as if teetering on the brink of collapse. Although it was winter, bright geraniums flowered on sills beside shuttered windows. We passed a swathe of charred land punctuated by coils of violet smoke. The air smelled of burning timber at this site of a recent fire.

The car lurched around a corner and almost collided with an ivy-covered wall beyond which was a ruined building, its arched doors and windows boarded with planks.

"What's that?" said John.

"It was the church of Pammakaristos," said Mr. Stathis, "a fine example of Byzantine architecture. When the barbarians conquered our city it became the mosque of Fethiye."

"Byzantine, of course," John said, rolling down the window. "Let's take a closer look."

"Alas, sir," said Mr. Stathis, "we Christians cannot enter the grounds of the mosque without permission from the appropriate ministry."

"No one will object if I examine the outer walls," said John, starting out of the car.

"Be careful, John," said Connie. "Don't want to anger the locals."

"I'm not going to trample sacred ground." I noticed an edge of impatience in his tone. I followed Stathis and John out of the car.

"It is said this church was built by Emperor John Comemnos to celebrate the conquest of Istanbul."

John whistled under his breath. "These stones must be centuries old."

"Eight or nine hundred years of age—no one knows for sure. We Greeks have been living here for centuries, long before the barbarians came," whispered Stathis. "Now their empire is defeated, and this land will soon be ours once more."

"Do you really believe that?" said John.

"It is just a matter of time, sir. Lloyd George himself has promised the Haghia Sophia will be returned to the orthodox church."

"The Allied leaders are inundated with demands. There is much to be taken care of in Paris."

"We Greeks have faith that our needs are high on the agenda."

"How can you be so sure?"

"Lloyd George is a Hellenist, sir," said Stathis in a firm voice, "educated in the classical tradition, conversant in Greek and Latin as is the custom in the civilized countries of Europe."

John noticed I was watching their discussion and gave me a wry smile.

My eye rested on a square house set back from the street. A screen covering a ground floor window closed as if one of the occupants had been watching us. Moments later the door opened and a bearded man in flowing green robes hurried down the path, his turban tilted to one side as if he had put it on in a hurry.

"An imam, sir, an elder of the mosque. Leave him to me. I know how to talk to these people."

19

The stranger had a mellifluous voice. He leaned toward Mr. Stathis, gesticulating and pointing at the car.

"He says these ruins are unsafe," said Stathis. "I explained you are an important American diplomat, so he offered to show us the mosque of Suleimaniye, a short drive from here."

"Suleimaniye. Heck told me it is a masterpiece, not to be missed."

"Very unusual for an imam to invite nonbelievers to a mosque, sir."

"You have brought us luck, Mary." John flashed a radiant smile.

The chauffeur opened the car door, but John expressed a desire to walk. The imam declined our offer of a seat in the front of the car, so the two of them strode away while Mr. Stathis followed several paces behind. When I climbed back into the car, Connie seemed bewildered. She threaded her fingers through mine and stared out of the window, not saying a word. In a matter of minutes we had lost sight of the men as our car slowed to a crawl in the maze of back streets.

We found John standing under an arched gateway looking animated, while the imam waited a few feet away.

"This is highly irregular, sir. We can't just walk into a mosque," said Mr. Stathis.

"He seems to be inviting us," said John.

"I cannot enter a Muslim place of worship."

"Do you mean to tell me you have never been into a mosque?"

"Never, sir, nor will I."

"These people have been your neighbors for centuries. Aren't you curious to see their places of worship?"

"Speaking for myself, sir," Mr. Stathis dropped his voice, " I find it expedient to remain."

"I will take my chances. You stay here with Connie and Mary," said John.

"No," I exclaimed reaching for the door handle. "Not missing this opportunity."

The men hesitated; the imam pointed to my hat. I removed the pins, tossed it in the back seat and pulled my shawl tightly around my face.

"Madame," said Mr. Stathis as I started after John, "don't reveal so much hair."

I was conscious of many pairs of eyes watching us as we made our way along the gravel path. As the imam swept by, the men pressed their hands together in a gesture of prayer. The women's entrance was guarded by a girl with darting eyes who thrust a pair of oversized slippers at me. When she pulled aside the oilcloth curtain I found myself in an enclosure marked off from the main part of the mosque by a carved balustrade. The beauty of the interior astonished me. It was unlike anything I had seen before. It took a moment for my eyes to adjust to the half-light. Vast domes, tiered one upon another, created an impression of soaring space. The air was dense, permeated with the smell of incense and burning oil drifting from a circle of lamps suspended from the ceiling by slender chains. Standing beneath the apex of the central dome, I watched the light filtering in through arched windows set high in the outer wall. When the sun shifted, shadows flickered across the glowing walls, and specks of dust danced on the rays.

At the base of one of the giant pillars sat a group of women, heads bent, turning prayer beads between their fingers. Something in the twisting of those beads struck a chord of recognition in me. The ceaseless circle, round and round—the eternal nature of being. I bowed my head and murmured a prayer in the solitary peace of the mosque, where centuries of worship had left an imprint on the air. The imam placed his fingers against his chin and smiled; separated by the gulf of language, I could do nothing more than stare around in wonder.

Close to four the light began to fade; the impending curfew was upon us. John sat up front with the chauffeur, and Connie and I in the back, separated from the men by a sliding panel. When I told my sister about my experience of recognition, she cut me short.

"Do not be deceived," she said quietly. "This tranquility is all on the surface. Underneath the Turks possess a churning violence. You see it in their eyes. Oh, yes—they stand back, they bow when we pass, but their eyes shift; they watch everything. I shudder to imagine the nature of the god they worship."

"Where did you get such ideas?"

"We read of their atrocities in London. The daily papers were full of news of the Armenian massacres," she whispered, casting a look at John's back. "I know for a fact all the Unitarian churches in America collected money to help those hapless Christian souls."

"I've never heard you talk this way. What's come over you?"

"Our country was founded on Christian principles; my husband is a representative here for everything the United States stands for," she replied primly. "Don't get carried away with the exotic foreignness of this city, Mary. You've suffered a terrible loss, and you are vulnerable."

# 3

Palazzo Corpi stood on a hill overlooking the Golden Horn, a stone's throw from the old Italian neighborhood of Galata. One afternoon about a month after my arrival, Connie and I decided to explore the area. We wandered past grandiose apartment buildings that soared above the narrow streets like canyon walls. On and on down the hill we went toward the water. The grandeur gave way to tenements, and an open drain gushed over the cobbles. Connie stopped as an old woman hobbled past, shoving us to one side with a deft thrust of her elbow. Tiny, almost dwarf-like, she turned her head, and her black eyes flashed. She opened her mouth, revealing toothless gums, and from the back of her throat came a squawk, like a parrot. She shook her stick at us and then hobbled away. We watched until she disappeared into a side street.

"We should not go any farther," said Connie. "I get the feeling we are not welcome."

"Did you see her face? What an amazing subject. Wish I had my sketchbook here. I left it in my room."

"Can you memorize her features?"

"It's not the same," I said.

"Let's go back."

"Why, Connie? We've scarcely started out."

"John doesn't know we are here. I have always stayed in Pera."

"Those old streets look so inviting."

"It's not New York, Mary. The situation here is fragile. That old woman was not happy to see us. They don't like Westerners, not after the defeat." She tapped her hat as if to emphasize our foreign appearance.

Something in her tone stopped me from pressing the subject any further. An idea had been planted, my curiosity roused. The women around me covered their heads; their scarves afforded anonymity. This was a Muslim *mahalle*, and I was the interloping stranger easily identified by my cloche hat and calf-length coat.

Tossing her head, Connie led the way up the hill; panting, she hurried along the center of the street to avoid the crowds.

In New York, in what seemed like another life, I had been a painter. My subjects were the immigrant women who lived and worked in the crowded tenements of the Lower East Side. My palette was dark, my canvases claustrophobic, reflecting the conditions I painted. I soon earned a reputation for the "savage" honesty of my work. I had several shows at the Macbeth Gallery and gradually made a name for myself. My most controversial canvas showed a teenage seamstress stretched out on a bed, exhausted after a day at the sweatshop. Her legs were splayed, her mouth open as if she were crying out in ecstasy or pain. Her posture was deliberately ambiguous. The collector Gertrude Vanderbilt Whitney bought the painting.

Burnham was one of the realists who shocked the New York art world with his paintings of the harsh world of the immigrants and the poor.

We met at an art opening when I was barely out of my teens. I fell instantly and hopelessly in love the moment I laid eyes on him. His looks have been described as exotic: olive skin, dark blond hair, and slanting blue eyes inherited from his English mother, a governess who met her husband, an Italian carpenter, on the Staten Island ferry. Like his father he was small, with the compact body of a Sicilian worker.

Aside from his unusual looks the most appealing thing about Burnham was his confidence; Burnham painted only to please himself, careless of the opinions of critics and collectors. His gift was undeniable—he worked hard and built a reputation that assured his place in the New York panoply of the so-called avant-garde. In those days I was a first year student at the art students league, the bottom rung, motivated by the naïve desire to express myself. Burnham was my first and only lover. He took my work seriously and encouraged me as both a painter and an artist. The combination was potent. Less than a year after our initial encounter I ran away to live with him. My flight caused a scandal; the news even made its way into the papers in those innocent far-off days before the war.

By the end of 1916 war had been raging in Europe for three long years. Despite German provocation, President Wilson hesitated to intervene; America was prospering, the economy growing fast thanks to the influx of immigrant labor. Bit by bit the mournful news from England trickled in: Burnham's English cousin Freddy killed at sea, then Thomas and Edward, dead in the trenches. Burnham's anger burned like a slow flame. He echoed Teddy Roosevelt's outrage: Wilson was a coward; it was the moral duty of America to go to Britain's aid. He stopped painting and joined the war lobby in Washington.

Finally, when he could stand it no longer, he set sail for England and with the help of an uncle, enlisted in the English army. Trying to talk him out of it would have been pointless. A few days before his departure we got married in a brief ceremony at city hall. We returned to our apartment on Tenth Street and lived intensely from day to day, not daring to talk of the future. In July 1916 Burnham perished in a cloud of mustard gas at the Battle of the Somme.

When the telegram came, the protective shell cracked, and through the jagged wound I glimpsed infinity. Time became an enemy The days ran into one another with relentless monotony. I stopped painting; my art, once an act of love, seemed pointless. Throughout that dreadful winter I did not leave our apartment. I stayed close to what remained of Burnham, breathing the lingering smell of his clothes hanging in the closet, running my hand over the bristles of the shaving brush that once touched his cheek. No one was allowed to move his possessions; everything had to stay as it had been when he was alive.

When spring came I ventured no farther than my parents' home a few blocks away. Our apartment had become both prison and refuge. I was safe, yet trapped; an imprint of Burnham's absence was burned into the air. Walking was a solace that became a daily obsession; in the streets of the city I was never alone. I walked and walked, back and forth across the Brooklyn Bridge, uptown to Central Park, down to Broadway, through the Lower East Side, Little Italy, and on to the docks. Neither weather nor time of day deterred me. Walking was a way of being alone with my thoughts, alone with the gradual realization that Burnham was never coming back. How strange that life went on while Burnham languished in eternity.

It was late January when I arrived in Paris, and I had no desire to linger. In the half-light of rosy dawn my driver and I headed north; it wasn't long before the nightmarish scenario began to unfold. Mile upon mile of gentle hills had been transformed into a swamp. Once-idyllic pastureland was now an endless ocean of mud crisscrossed by hellish wire and trenches overflowing with filthy water, turned to ice in the bitter wind. It was hard to imagine the piles of rubble and brick had once been villages and the jagged arches were all that remained of medieval churches blown apart by artillery fire.

According to the State Department, Burnham's body was buried about half a mile outside the town of Albert. The cemetery stood beside a crossroads in what had once been a wheat field. Row upon row of dark wooden crosses marked the closely packed graves that stretched, four deep, for half a mile or more along the side of the road. Wisps of wild grass had begun to sprout over the mounds where the dead lay. With tears in his eyes the old man assigned to be my guide told me villagers came weekly to tend the graves.

When I found Burnham's name a familiar emptiness washed over me. I lay face down on the mound of earth, but the soil was iron hard and would not yield to my body. Poor Burnham, immortalized in my memory, wrenched violently from the life he loved. I began to weep, not just for my loss but for all the work left unfinished—paintings that would never be done. My body shuddered as once it had shaken with the passion of lovemaking. Burnham was dead; I had seen his grave; it was true.

# 4

"Allah Ekhber, Allah, Allah."

The cry of the *muezzin* penetrated every street close to the great mosque of Yeni Cami. It echoed from the walls and swirled along the narrow alleys calling the people back to prayer. Since noon I had been wandering through the crowded markets making quick drawings of tired faces, trying to capture the melancholy that permeated this part of town. With my head covered in a traditional woolen shawl, no one gave me a second glance. This simple disguise allowed me to move freely within the old Muslim neighborhoods. How naïve I was, unaware of the tensions between the many disparate cultures thrown together in the seething city.

The call to prayer reminded me the afternoon was drawing to a close. A west wind blew up and whipped over the cobbles. I quickened my pace; within an hour it would be dark. That night there was to be a reception for the Swedish ambassador. Admiral Bristol's wife was still in America, so Connie had been asked to act as hostess. Feelings of guilt tinged my dread at the prospect of attending a diplomatic reception. What had I expected?

The last tram to Galata was supposed to leave an hour before sunset. In those days schedules were nonexistent. Trams and ferries came and

29

went with insouciance that bordered on anarchy, a symptom of the general air of uncertainty that pervaded Istanbul at that time. I noticed a lone tram idling on the far side of Eminonu square, an unruly crowd of women pressed around the entry where a grim-faced conductor stood astride the platform waving his fists like a prizefighter. Passengers pressed their faces against the steamy windows gazing at the fracas. The more the women pushed forward, shifting their baskets like battering rams, the more agitated the conductor became.

Pulling my shawl tightly around me, I moved closer, praying no one would notice me. The conductor turned, a bell clanged, the driver locked into gear, and the tram shuddered forward, provoking screams of rage. In the confusion an elderly woman fell; I was close enough to hear the thud as her body hit the ground. Her basket rolled under the tram. Frustrated, the driver leaned across the wheel, hurling insults through his open window. Heads turned, all eyes focused toward the new confrontation. Temporarily distracted, the conductor stepped into the street. Clutching my bag close to my body, I hopped onto the platform and slipped into the women's section only to find every bench filled. Even the center aisle was crammed with passengers.

Toward the center of the car a small woman in a tweed suit was perched on the edge of her seat. A light veil covered the lower half of her face, and a second, darker, scarf was thrown back over her head. As I drew close she looked bewildered, as if she knew me. Putting her finger to her lips she slid along the bench, making a sliver of space where I sat down, still holding my bag. Without thinking I murmured a word of thanks.

My relief was short lived. The conductor pushed his way through the women in the aisle, his face contorted with anger. He stopped in front of me, berating me, spittle flying, eyes narrowed. Keeping my gaze down, I refused to move. The conductor caught hold of my shoulder and dug his fingers into my flesh. The woman beside me tensed. The conductor tightened his grip. He had strong hands, and streaks of pain shot down my back. I was conscious that the women around me were silent; no one moved. Possessed by a primal sense of self-preservation, I lifted my arm and drove my clenched fist between his legs. The punch was so hard I scraped my knuckles against the coarse fabric of his trousers. He felt soft like sponge. He fell back against the women crowded behind him.

The next thing I knew the curtain separating us from the men's section was ripped aside and a leather-faced stranger stepped into the cabin waving a pistol above his head. He wore a tattered khaki coat with a line of gilded medals that clanked when he lowered the pistol and pointed it at the conductor, who scrambled to his feet and stumbled back to the safety of his platform as the stranger turned to follow. A bell rang and the tram lurched forward, slowly at first, then gathering speed. I saw the conductor standing in the square, head bowed, clutching his groin. We raced across the Galata Bridge and through the empty streets. I hugged my bag to stop myself from shaking. I was still trembling when we pulled into Tunel Square and barely made it down the steps into the street.

"If it had not been for that old soldier, I dread to think what might have happened," said a voice. Close behind me stood the woman in the tweed suit.

"You speak English?"

"You pretend to be a Turk, so you must understand the danger. Those women were Greek. They hate us."

"The conductor?"

"Another Greek, more hatred." She lowered her voice. Across the square a soldier was watching us from a doorway.

"We must go; the hour is late," she said before I had a chance to ask more questions.

I turned into an arcade, still shaken by the incident on the bus. Why were the Turks treated as outcasts in their own city, I wondered. What prompted such hatred between people who had lived side by side for centuries? A single gas lamp burned in a bracket on the wall, its light barely penetrating the darkness. In New York City the night streets were bright with the fire of electricity, but here in Istanbul the night was dark as Hades. I hurried on, pulling my shawl over my head as if to protect myself.

The passage tapered to a flight of steps leading to a square where five roads converged. The familiar streets had been transformed into shadowy canyons. Disoriented, I paused, wondering which way to go. By now I was worried—I was going to be late for the reception. A stranger dashed out of the shadows. He wore a fez with a tassel that swung back and forth and shone in the lamplight. I drew back, but my movement caught his eye and he turned to look at me. He must have been about seventeen, a trace of a moustache on his upper lip. Perspiration trickled down his cheeks, and his eyes brimmed with tears. For what seemed like an eternity we faced one another. Behind us, from the covered passage, came the sound of footsteps.

"Where did he go?" said an English voice.

"Down there."

"Silly young fool—why did he run away?"

Reaching into the folds of his coat the young man pulled out a sheaf of papers and thrust them toward me. Terrified, I backed away. Then I heard a click, and when he pushed the papers at me, this time with more force, I did something in that split second that was to change my life forever. Pulling open my bag, I took the documents and shoved them between the leaves of my drawing pad.

"*Holiday hanoom*," he whispered, his voice cracking with urgency. "*Holiday hanoom*."

I nodded, and anger welled up inside me—the proximity of the enemy; the smell of fear. Is this what Burnham felt close to the end?

Pressing his hands together at his chest the man bowed, an automatic gesture of good manners that touched me even as I trembled with fear. He turned and ran into the open square. Sliding into the shadows, I watched as a pair of soldiers in red jackets appeared at the top of the steps, their rifles drawn.

"There he is," said the taller of the two.

"Stop—put your hands up."

"He doesn't speak English."

"He knows there is a curfew."

At that moment another patrol dressed in khaki appeared at the far end of the square. There were three of them bunched together, rifles at the ready. The young Muslim was trapped.

"What's going on?" said an English voice.

"He's a suspect," said the soldier in red. "We've followed him from the docks."

"Want us to arrest him?"

"No, he's ours. We'll take it from here."

Trapped, the boy glanced behind him, his face taut with fear. He stood frozen to the spot. Suddenly he bolted toward a dark street. The second patrol dropped to their knees and let fly a volley of bullets. A piercing scream ripped through the air. I turned away and flattened my face against the wall. My knees buckled and I tore at the stone with my fingernails for fear of collapsing.

Behind me I heard a gasp, then a shot, and another, and another. The air filled with the smell of smoke.

"What the hell have you done?"

There was a jangle of artillery as the soldiers in red thudded down the steps, passing so close I felt the air move.

"Who is that man? He didn't have to kill him like a dog."

Swept by nausea, I lifted my hand to my mouth. The touch of my palm was startling, as if a stranger was trying to gag me.

"Your man was getting away." The voice was rough, with a hint of an accent—Scots perhaps?

"You bloody murdered him."

"I'll have you arrested for insubordination."

"You aren't my sergeant. You'll be in trouble once HQ gets to hear of it."

"Self-defense—the man was going to shoot me."

My knees buckled and my body brushed against the wall, sending crumbs of stone skittering across the street.

"What was that?"

"Came from over there, sir."

"It's a Turkish woman." A soldier started toward me.

My hand reached out, blocking his path, and from deep within came a voice I did not recognize.

"Don't touch me," I said. Tugging at my scarf, I held it tight as my hair fell ragged over my shoulders. "I'm American. Don't come near me."

He hesitated, glancing nervously at the street where the body lay inert, splayed on the cobbles like a broken puppet. Close by, his fez had rolled into the gutter, the glittering tassel submerged in a pool of blood. The sight provoked a sadness so heavy it displaced the horror, as if my conscious mind could not take it in.

His killer was still standing over him, pistol clutched in his right hand. He was puffy faced, with tight lips and ears that stuck out like flaps. On his arm his rank was picked out in gold—sergeant's stripes. When he turned his eyes on me they seemed to swim out of focus, as if fixed on a distant point beyond my head.

"What is an American doing out after curfew?" he hissed

"I was lost."

"But you just happened to be in the same vicinity as a known criminal," he said, jutting his chin toward the body.

Mute from fear, I did not respond.

34

"Why should I believe you?" His words slowed, like a phonograph winding down. "For all I know you're an accomplice."

The soldiers stood around in a semicircle, shuffling their feet.

"I saw her get off the tram, sergeant. She was talking to another woman."

The sergeant took a step closer. "Give me your name," he whispered.

"Mary."

"Mary what?"

"My brother is an important official at the American Consulate. He will vouch for me."

A frown flitted across his face. Sliding the pistol back into his holster, the sergeant stared at the ground. Seconds dragged by.

"Tompkins, get over here." Jerking his head he barked a command at the soldiers standing nearby. "See that road? It leads to the American Consulate. Don't let this woman out of your sight 'til she is inside the gates."

I went to retrieve my bag, lying on the ground in the arch where I had concealed myself.

"Not so fast. Let me take a look at that." Arm outstretched, he made a move to take my bag, but a soldier in the other company prevented him.

"Be careful, Sergeant. Diplomatic immunity — might create an international incident, and you have enough problems."

The sergeant hesitated, then waved me away. Holding tight to my bag, I followed Tompkins down the darkened road. We passed close to the dead man. His blood had started to dry, forming deep red pools in the cracks between the cobbles.

# 5

The streets were dark. Overhead a ribbon of navy sky was visible between the buildings. When we rounded a corner a blaze of light flooded over the cobbles, and our shadows stretched behind us like wandering ghosts. The gates of the Palazzo Corpi were open, and every window of the palazzo burned with the glow of chandeliers. Tompkins stopped, his face shining in the golden light.

"I'd forget what you saw, ma'am," he whispered.

"How do you know what I saw, Tompkins?"

"He's mad. Put it out of your mind."

He averted his eyes, and my questioning look went unheeded. The consulate guards snapped their heels and lifted their arms in an abrupt salute as I walked to the foot of the steps, safe once more on American ground. Still tense from fear, I ran up the steps clutching my bag. Tompkins lingered by the gate watching until I disappeared from view.

The main hall had been transformed. The mountain of boxes and trunks had vanished and in their place stood long tables shrouded in white cloths and set with silverware, glasses, and pyramids of dried fruit on glass dishes. Lights burned from every bracket. No one was around. I felt a surge of relief.

From a distant room piano music flooded into the hall—a Beethoven sonata played with such passion it stopped me in my tracks. A door opened and Connie appeared, her beaded dress shimmering in the light, her face glistening with anticipation.

"Thank God you're back. Where were you? I've been worried sick."

"I'm sorry, I'm sorry, Connie," I managed in a strained whisper. "The last tram to Galata was delayed and the streets were so dark I got lost."

She seized my arm as if to guide me along the corridor. "It's dangerous to be out at this hour. Why, you're shaking! What's the matter?"

"I'm not used to running." No point in revealing the truth, not now. I had to gather my thoughts, think carefully. The music surged again. "Who is playing? They are very gifted."

"Mikhail something, an exile. John heard him at one of these new Russian restaurants; he earns his keep playing for the customers, but who appreciates classical music in this godforsaken city?"

Behind us car doors slammed and voices came from the drive. Connie glanced around.

"They can't be here already; it's too early. The invitation said eight o'clock."

"Go and greet your guests. I can find my way upstairs. I must go and dress."

"You look exhausted, Mary. Don't feel you have to come. There will be more parties," she said.

"I *am* tired," I said, making no attempt to conceal my relief.

"The ambassador is bringing his niece. We only just received word of the addition, so we'll need an extra space at dinner." She kissed my cheek and ushered me toward the back stairs. As the doors swung shut behind me the music faded, like smoke vanishing in an autumn sky.

I dropped onto the bed, relieved to be alone and quiet; the shock of the murder was just starting to sink in, and the last thing I wanted was to make small talk with the myriad guests assembling three floors below me. I removed my clothes and tossed them in a corner, where they lay in a rumpled pile contaminated by the horror I felt. I vowed never to wear them again. Wrapping myself in a warm robe, I unclasped my bag and removed the sketchbook, taking care not to let the papers slip from between the leaves of drawings. One by one I placed them on my bed: more than fifty sheets of cream vellum the texture of velvet covered in Arabic script. The manuscript must have been written by a skilled draftsman, for the penmanship was flawless—not a slip, not a blot—the work of a master. What was it, I wondered—a religious text, political, or one of the long, triumphant poems so beloved by the Ottomans? Where was the man taking them at that late hour, and why were the British pursuing him with such deadly intent?

As if in a dream I took my pad and placed it across my knees. I have no memory of picking up the charcoal. With swift, decisive strokes I rendered the body, the pool of blood, and the fez lying on its side in the gutter. The drawings poured out in clear images—that last beseeching look and the way his brow furrowed before he turned away, urgently imploring, "*Holiday hanoom, holiday hanoom.*" Although the memory was clear, the drawings came from a place beyond my consciousness.

The front door slammed as someone came into the hall. I heard Connie's voice calling for me the way she did when we were children in the house on Tenth Street, the bereft little sister always in search of her elusive playmate, for her games bored me and I rarely answered her call. I gathered the papers and sketches and shoved them under some clothes at the bottom of a drawer. Wrapping myself in a robe, I tiptoed to the door and looked out.

"I'm up here."

"Are you all right? You looked so distraught I've been worried."

"I was tired," I said, conscious my body was still shaking.

"Did you have supper? I can send a servant up with food."

"I'm not hungry."

"How about hot milk?"

"Nothing, my dear. I'm about to have a bath and sleep."

"If you are sure ..." her voice wavered with uncertainty.

"Go back to your guests. John will be wondering where you are."

The gas heater was broken and I had to make do with splashing dregs of lukewarm water over my face and rubbing my skin with one of the soft cotton towels embroidered with an American eagle. My body cleansed, my mind churned as I lay on the bed. I could not shake the image of that pleading face. Why had they killed him? Why, why?

Gradually I drifted into a restless sleep, but peace was denied to me, even in my dreams. I returned to the primeval forest where I had wandered in my sleep in the months after Burnham died. The air was hot and humid, water dripped from the trees, and fronds of lush ferns brushed against my bare legs as I pushed my way through the dense undergrowth. Suddenly there was a path, and the jungle vanished, giving way to the calm green hillsides of New England. Burnham hurried over the crest of a hill; in his outstretched hand he held a sheaf of papers. They were telegrams, all printed with the same message.

"We regret to inform you that your husband, Captain Burnham Di Benedetti, was killed by enemy fire September 1916 during the Battle of the Somme." When I looked up, Burnham had vanished.

I woke with a start, my body drenched with sweat. In the street a car door slammed, and someone cried out that the tire had burst.

For a moment I forgot where I was; then the events of the evening crowded back and I sat up, my heart pounding. Wrapping myself in a shawl, I sat by the open window. The plaintive wail of an imam drifted across the rooftops, then another and another, the rondo of voices flooding the room. Cool night air blew against my face. With unexpected force, desire I thought long buried overcame me. I wanted nothing more than to wake beside Burnham and hold him close again. Then the cacophony subsided and quiet descended on the city. Pink light spread across the sky and faded to white. I threw myself back on the bed and slipped once more into the half sleep of tangled dreams.

Hours later I was woken by Connie shaking my shoulder.

"Wake up, dear. Admiral Bristol wants to see you," she said. I tried to read the look on her face, but in my fog of sleep its meaning eluded me. "John is waiting downstairs. He'll go with you to Bristol's office."

"This request from Bristol is unusual. I didn't even know he was aware you were here," said John. He was treating me with such tenderness that I felt a wave of guilt.

"I think I know the reason. Last night I was witness to a dreadful scene—dreadful—a chance encounter with British troops when I was on my way home."

"Home from where? Where were you? What are you talking about?"

"I saw a murder, by British soldiers. I mean no, the soldiers didn't kill him; it was one man, a sergeant."

"A murder?" He stopped at the foot of the stairs.

"I don't know where to start."

Evoked by the memory, a wave of nausea swept through me. I leaned against the balustrade to steady myself.

"Sit down, Mary." He leaned forward and caught me by the arm. "You've gone white. Do you want some water?"

"No, I must tell you everything before we see the admiral."

Words poured out of me, every excruciating detail, save for one—I said nothing about the papers. John put his large hand over mine and squeezed my fingers between his.

"Why did you keep this to yourself?" he said gently.

"When I reached the consulate your guests were arriving. The reception meant so much to Connie and I didn't want to spoil it for her, so I went to my room."

He shook his head. "The Allies have a rogue soldier in their ranks. Now they know you are a witness."

"I am sorry, John. This places you in a difficult position."

"Let's hear what the admiral has to say. I barely know him, but by all accounts he is a fair-minded man who is not biased one way or the other."

I followed John through the maze of corridors that led to the annex where Admiral Bristol had set up his offices. It was a relief to understand that John's brusque and certain manner had mellowed.

The admiral was waiting for us. I was surprised to find he was only a few inches taller than I; I had anticipated a towering figure. Years at sea had left him with a ruddy complexion and creases at the corners of his eyes that deepened when he smiled. His upright bearing lent him an air of authority at odds with his amiable expression.

"Mrs. Di Benedetti," he said, extending his hand toward me. "Forgive me for disturbing you at such an early hour, but the matter is urgent."

With a fatherly air he ushered the two of us toward a pair of sofas that faced one another across a low table. He waved his hand above tray a set with a coffee pot, cups, and a plate of pastries. "Not much of a breakfast—this is all the kitchen could muster."

"Shall I pour?" I asked after an awkward pause.

"The British Secret Service were here this morning," said the admiral, looking me straight in the eye. "They demanded an interview with you, Mrs. Di Benedetti. No reason given. I refused, of course—damned nerve. If the Allies want to interview an American in the confines of the American Consulate, they know perfectly well they must give a reason."

"The British can be arbitrary in their dealings with our consulate," said John, leaning forward and resting his elbows on his knees.

"My old friend Colonel Heathcote Smythe is stationed here." The admiral reached for a cup and took a sip. "I called him and heard the full story—their version, of course; there's always another point of view."

So he knew. This was surprise, yet a relief.

"I am curious to hear if your version of events coincides with the British."

Taking care to recall every detail, I repeated what I had told John. All the while I was conscious that the admiral watched every change of expression on my face.

"You are certain he was shot without provocation," he said, shaking his head.

"I didn't see the shooting, and I don't know why he was running, but the other soldiers were horrified. I overheard them talking."

"Statements to that effect were taken from the other witnesses."

"No need for Mary to be subjected to an interrogation," said John, laying a hand on my arm. "She has told you all she knows, haven't you, Mary?"

I nodded.

"A written statement will suffice," said Admiral Bristol. "Have it on my desk by the end of the week. I will tell the British to let the matter rest."

"Does this mean I don't have to talk to them?"

"For the foreseeable future, but my jurisdiction is limited. I can protect you for just so long. From now on stay in the European area and wear your own clothes. No more disguises, no more veils and cloaks."

"How can I observe street life in the old city unless I am covered and inconspicuous?" I protested.

"Forget this fascination with the Turkish neighborhoods. If you will forgive my saying so, your romanticism is both naïve and misplaced."

"For an artist naïveté can be a blessing. My disguises, such as they are, provide cover for observation; we artists are trained to observe."

He fixed me with a studied gaze as if seeing me for the first time. "You may be mistress of your own destiny, but as an American in Asia Minor your safety is my responsibility."

As the mantel clock struck nine, its strident chimes rang around the room like a peal of bells.

"Time is passing, Mrs. Di Benedetti. If you will excuse me, I have work to do."

The interview was over. As he squeezed my hand in a gesture of farewell, I had the uneasy feeling he knew I was hiding something.

# 6

That afternoon Connie and I took a walk along the Grande Rue de Péra, through the European quarter, to Les Jardins de Taxim, a Parisian-style park built on the site of a graveyard. We approached La Grande Maison de Couture, an imposing edifice of gilt and glass, standing on the corner of the Grande Rue and Imam Hassan sokak. Improbable confections of taffeta, lace, and satin crowded the window. Close by, a line of men in ragged uniforms stood with metal trays slung around their necks crammed with trinkets, paper, flowers, combs, and discarded medals from forgotten wars.

"Refugees, White Russians," Connie whispered, looking at their cropped heads. "They were driven out by the Bolsheviks. There's a revolution going on up there."

Ships from the Black Sea arrived every day and disgorged their human cargo onto the docks at Hydar Pasha and Scutari where, it was said, Russian aristocrats tossed their furs and jewels from the boats in exchange for food.

"Don't get too close," cautioned my sister, tightening her grip on my arm. "There is a cholera epidemic in the refugee camps. It's not known except in diplomatic circles—the Allies don't want to create a panic."

An older man hovered on the edge of the group of Russians and snapped to attention as I approached his tray. While I picked out quill pens and a bottle of ink he stood straight, his eyes averted. As I counted the coins into his outstretched palm his eyes closed and he nodded, more from despair than gratitude.

Not far away a man in a checkered jacket leaned against the door, reading a newspaper. He glanced up, then returned to his paper. He looked up again and his mouth twitched in a half smile; carefully folding his paper, he slid it into his pocket and started to walk toward us. I realized with a start that it was the sergeant. Grabbing Connie by the arm, I pulled her to the center of the boulevard.

"What's the matter?" she said.

"Someone I must not see," I said, unwilling to frighten her.

We hurried toward Taxim Park. I felt borne along on the flow of people like flotsam on a fast-moving river. We passed cafés with gay striped awnings of pink and green and white, and stores crowded with shoppers. I saw a church set back from the road at the end of a darkened courtyard and sentries in scarlet uniforms guarding a mansion set behind curved iron gates. On we went, with the sergeant close behind us. Never had the Grande Rue seemed so long as it did that afternoon.

It was late in the afternoon and the tea rooms were busy. We entered one where well-dressed patrons were crowded together on velvet banquettes and gold-buttoned chairs. Cigar smoke clouded the air. But for the Orthodox priest sitting near the entrance, in flowing black robes with a heavy cross on his chest, we might have been in Paris or Vienna. Waiters in tails bobbed between the tables, their heads shiny with brilliantine. Some carried trays piled with sandwiches, cakes, and bowls filled with cream. The maître d'hôtel, in black tie and tails, led us to a table by the wall, away from the clamor.

"Who was that man?" said Connie, leaning across the table.

"I thought it was the sergeant from last night," I said quietly, pretending to study the menu. "I might be wrong. I only got a glimpse of him."

"My God, was he following us?" she hissed, her eyes wide.

"I don't know, I don't know," I said, picking up a napkin. Droplets of perspiration trickled down my forehead, and the air around me felt uncomfortably hot.

"Let me find you a handkerchief," said Connie, opening her bag.

The waiter coughed, as if to remind us he was still there, and I blushed under his disapproving gaze.

"We'll take the éclairs and the de chine," said Connie. She handed the menus to the waiter and waved her hand as if to dismiss him. "I'm sorry I invited you here, Mary. I thought it would help, but as it turns out, Istanbul is a dangerous place."

"Please don't apologize, Connie. With danger comes life and I am beginning to feel it stir within me again."

The waiter returned carrying a tray at shoulder level. We looked on in silence while he laid out the china and silver with meticulous care.

"Tell me about the reception; how did it go?" I said, eager to change the subject.

"Apparently the Swedish ambassador complimented John on the food and said it was the finest party he had attended this season." Her eyes glistened. "Even Admiral Bristol was impressed. He is not an easy man to please."

"You looked so beautiful, everyone must have been charmed."

"Did you like my dress? I had it made in London."

We fell into an easy conversation about the reception but skated over the surface, avoiding the dangerous waters lurking beneath the ice.

We failed to see an angular woman of unusual height making her way across the room toward our table.

"Mrs. Olsen?" The speaker craned forward and peered at Connie. I noticed her skin was weather-worn like that of a farmer or country woman. "Forgive me—my lorgnette is in my bag."

"Miss Billings," said Connie rising from her seat. "I thought you were in Konya."

"Annie and I returned two days ago. The situation in the interior is becoming impossible We desperately need supplies for our orphanages."

"May I introduce my sister, Mary. She arrived from New York a few weeks ago."

"Oh, my dear," said Miss Billings. She clasped my hand and her gray eyes flashed with concern. "Admiral Bristol told me what happened. I am so sorry you had to witness such a horrible incident."

"I didn't see anything."

"Annie and I were saying only yesterday how conditions have worsened in Istanbul; the Allies are tightening the noose. Don't they know the war is over? They won, if you can call the sacrifice of several million lives a victory." She shivered and stiffened as if a cold wind had blown past her. I liked her at once.

"If I had known you were here I would have invited you to last night's reception," said Connie, who never discussed politics and rarely expressed an opinion unless it coincided with her husband's.

"Another time," said Miss Billings, waving brightly. "Maybe you can do something for Near East Relief—help us kindle interest in our work."

"Are you leaving? May we give you a lift? John has sent the consulate car to meet us. I could not face the long walk back at the end of the afternoon when the streets are crowded with workers."

"No, thank you, Mrs. Olsen. I don't mind the crowds."

Beyond the window daylight was fading. While Connie was preoccupied talking to the waiter, I glanced toward the window and noticed a man standing still in the midst of the bustling throng flowing along the sidewalk. He pressed his forehead against the glass, blinkered his eyes with his hands, and peered inside. From where I was sitting I could just make out a checkered jacket with a newspaper in the pocket; I shifted on the banquette so my back was turned toward him. I said nothing to Connie; the consulate car would be waiting to sweep us to safety once more.

Two days later I retreated to my studio with my pastels and a sketchbook. From my window I saw the clouds were low, and land and water seemed to melt together, as in a Turner seascape. When the winds swirled off the hills, the mist cleared, revealing the silhouettes of Allied battleships moored in the dark water. I tried to translate these impressions onto the pages of my sketchbook, but the mist shifted and the outlines changed, and I returned to my studies of the hamals, the human cargo carriers who worked on the docks. I first came across these men in the shadow of the Byzantine wall behind the Galata Tower. They were sleeping on a grassy knoll, huddled together for warmth. The cry of the muezzin disturbed them. Stretching like dogs, they shouldered their loads and with sure steps made their way down the precipitous hill, bent double beneath the weight of their cargo.

From that day on I watched them from a distance, making sketches, distilling my impressions, planning the arrangement of my first painting since Burnham's death.

Suddenly I was disturbed by raised voices coming from John's office.

"Olsen tells me the British were here." It was Lewis Heck. "Why wasn't I informed?"

"I wanted to interview her alone, gauge her character." Admiral Bristol's voice was distinctive; he always spoke as if issuing a command.

I had been so absorbed in my work I had not heard them come in. I crept over to the door, curious to hear what was being said.

"This Turkish resistance is becoming a nuisance again; the Allies have to keep order," said Heck.

"The incident contravenes the terms of the Hague Treaty and was witnessed by an American. We simply cannot let it pass." The admiral sounded angry.

"There are diplomatic procedures. Protocol governs the way we act, Admiral, not you."

"I do not trust the Allies. I deal directly with Heathcote Smythe. I know where I am with him."

"Just so you know where you are with me."

"Gentlemen, gentlemen," said John," please, let calm heads prevail."

"I don't want this incident to get blown out of proportion," said Bristol. "It's obvious your sister-in-law accidentally stumbled into something unsavory the British want kept under wraps."

"According to Allied headquarters the victim was a wanted man, a Nationalist," Heck went on.

"How do we know? Have the Allied authorities offered proof of these claims?"

"He belonged to a secret cell which has been plotting against the sultan's government. They had him under surveillance for several weeks."

"The Allies see conspiracy everywhere," said the admiral. "They're covering themselves, Heck. They've got a rogue soldier in their ranks and they don't want to admit it."

"I am duty bound to report this incident to Washington."

"My office submits daily reports to the State Department; the matter is already taken care of," said the admiral, clearing his throat.

"That's that then, isn't it," said Heck. "If you will excuse me, gentlemen, I have work to do."

A door slammed, chairs scraped across the floor.

"Heck is not a well man, sir," said John. "The weight of this assignment is taking its toll."

"Can't think why the State Department sent him here in the first place. Too junior to run a consulate."

"He knows the territory."

"Pah. He's as closed minded as the rest of them," said Bristol. "Listen, Olsen, this tour of inspection in the Black Sea will take weeks. While I'm gone keep an eye on Mary; we haven't heard the end of this."

Someone else entered the room; I heard the clack of heels.

"What is it, Miss Harrison?"

"Excuse me, sir, I didn't know the admiral was here."

Their voices faded, and John's response was lost in the clamor of a ship's horn echoing across the harbor.

# 7

In the middle of May the port of Smyrna was invaded by the Greeks; reports of fighting in the street reached our consulate. John did not understand why the Allies refused to intervene. Their ships lay at anchor offshore, within sight of the burning buildings. In Istanbul the Greek population was jubilant. Blue-and-white flags fluttered from their homes, and bells pealed in the towers of the Orthodox churches. Admiral Bristol had just returned from his tour, bringing with him a flotilla of destroyers and a battleship, the *Arizona*. They were anchored in the Horn, within sight of the consulate. This overt display of power troubled me. What use were they against the demoralized and increasingly melancholy population of refugees, demobilized soldiers, ragged children, and disenfranchised Turks who crowded the slums close to the docks?

More than six weeks had passed since the night of the murder, and the papers remained hidden in my drawer. What they were I did not know, and I had no idea how to dispose of them. The sergeant had disappeared, and I had resumed my daily excursions to the Old City. My heaviness had started to lift, but I recognized signs in others. There was a wariness now, in the gaze of the water carrier, the simit seller, the scribes huddled on the steps of the mosque. Their melancholy was tangible; it vibrated in the air like the held note of a violin.

Soon after the Smyrna debacle there was a reception at the palazzo for the educators from Robert College, the American School in Istanbul, and the American Girls College in Scutari. Close to seven o'clock I wandered onto the Chancery Terrace; in the valley below, gardens bloomed in every shade of green, pink, and white. In the distance the last blossoms of the Judas tree colored the hills a deep maroon. Seagulls wheeled above the waters of the Horn, which glowed silver green, like liquid mercury. The spectacle of spring made me feel alive.

I might have been in New York or Paris—there were elegant women in light chiffon and high heels, diplomatic wives, and professors from the Girls College in well-tailored flannel suits and shirts fastened at the neck, their no-nonsense hair scraped into knots at their necks. Men in uniform, others in frock coats, some with medals across their chests, boomed with knowing laughter. I had the impression that most of the guests knew one another.

At the far end of the terrace Miss Billings leaned against the wall staring into the evening sky. Her hair was piled in an untidy mass of curls. She wore a scarlet shawl embroidered with dragons and a pink satin dress. The effect was both chic and startling. Beside her a slender woman with a long nose and pale face sat at one of the flimsy tables. By contrast, her high collar and crisp white cuffs seemed old-fashioned. As I approached, she rose and introduced herself as Annie Allen, the head of Near East Relief.

"Your sister told me you were here for several months. You have chosen an interesting but unsettling time to come to this part of the world." I was struck by her low, pleasing voice; it contained a hint of an accent I could not place.

"I have already fallen under the spell of the place."

"Hauntingly beautiful location, no denying that. I have not yet adjusted to seeing Allied soldiers on every corner. An armed occupation is antithetical to the notion of a peace process, don't you agree, Billy?"

"Reminds me of the Crusades," said Miss Billings, drawing her shawl close round her shoulders. "Oh yes, Lloyd Gorge and Clemenceau talk easily of peace, but mark my words, they want to colonize all the land from here to Egypt."

"The admiral tells me you are a painter," said Miss Billings. "I was impressed to learn both you and your late husband were artistic innovators."

"How does he know? Did John tell him?" I said, startled.

"Mark Bristol is an intelligence officer," said Annie. "It is his business to know these things."

"We appreciate his open mind, but take care not to say too much in his presence," said Miss Billings with a smile.

A waiter passed with a tray of canapés; as he bent toward Miss Allen they exchanged a few words, and he bowed reverentially.

"Annie was born here. She speaks the language like a native," whispered Miss Billings.

"With a strong Anatolian accent, Florence; my Stamboulu friends constantly tease me."

"Annie's parents were missionaries in the East; they suffered under the old regime." Miss Billings took a sip from her glass.

"That was before the war, Billy. Those people are gone. By the grace of God I have survived to continue their work."

"Annie has an advantage over diplomats and the Allies, few of whom understand a word of Turkish."

"It will be their undoing. If people can't communicate, how can they hope to understand one another?" said Miss Allen.

The sky flashed turquoise and I shivered, caught in that mysterious moment between night and day. Lamps were lit, and the terrace was transformed into a blazing stage. I watched the players move back and forth smiling, laughing, fanning their faces as if they hadn't a care in the world. Miss Allen and Miss Billings rose and excused themselves in the same polite but firm voice. They reminded me of well-bred girls fresh out of finishing school. I was not alone for long.

"Mrs. Di Benedetti?" It was Admiral Bristol, radiating confidence in his dress uniform and gold-braided cap.

"Miss Allen was just talking about you," I said.

"Aha, you have made their acquaintance. Exceptional women, exceptional women. If the diplomatic community had one thousandth of their wisdom we would have a chance to achieve a measure of peace."

"I raise my glass to that," I replied.

"To Miss Allen and Miss Billings," said the admiral, "and all the strong and spirited women of America."

"On their behalf I accept your toast," I replied, emboldened by the champagne.

"I include the estimable Mrs. Bristol in that accolade; she is the best of her breed. There are plans for her to join me now I am settled on land. I'll miss my life on board ship. I have learned a lot about the East these past few months."

I was about to ask where he had been when a handsome man in a frock coat and fez hurried over to the admiral, his face creased with anxiety.

"I have been looking for you everywhere." He spoke with the inflections of a man trained at an English university.

"Dr. Adivar, what a surprise. I did not expect to see you here tonight."

"Halide and I would not refuse your kind invitation."

"This Smyrna business is appalling. Reports have been coming into my office all day. What is the prevailing mood of the cabinet?"

"Deep anger; we feel betrayed."

"If you have time, come to my office tomorrow. We must talk."

"My every movement is watched these days."

"Then the Allies know you are here."

"Yes, that is correct." Dr. Adnan Adivar sounded weary.

"Was your wife able to join us tonight?"

"I left her talking to Miss Allen. We did not know they were in town. I forgot their special border privileges."

"Why here she is — Halide Hanim, welcome. Let me introduce you to Mrs. Di Benedetti, a guest at the consulate."

"Did you say Halide Hanoom?" I asked, giving him a startled look.

"Hanim is equivalent to Mrs. or Madame."

*Halide Hanoom.* My head reeled, and their conversation evaporated like ether in air. I heard the voice of the dead man as clearly as if he were beside me again. "Holiday Hanoom." My glass fell from my hand and smashed on the hard stone, shattering into fragments. The three of them turned to look at me.

"It is possible you have eaten something that disagrees with you," said Dr. Adnan, "We will find a comfortable place to sit, and I will get a servant to bring water."

I was taken to a summer house in the lower garden, shaded by the branches of a large pine tree. The interior was cool and damp. Halide Hanim stayed with me, watching me from behind her veil; there was something dramatic about her silent presence. She reminded me of those spectral figures in the prints of Goya — half shadow, half human.

"I had a feeling we would meet again," she said.

Her voice was low and pleasing, with a slight hint of an American accent; I recognized it at once.

"The tram," I exclaimed.

"That was me," she said, unclipping her veil. She raised her head and gave me one of those quizzical looks I was to come to know so well. She was beautiful, but her beauty radiated from an inner force. Her nose was long, her brows heavy, her lips too full for her narrow chin. Nothing about her looks was conventional. Yet the intensity of her eyes distracted attention from the uneven arrangement of features. "I trust there is a consulate doctor who can take care of you."

"I am not sick."

"Then why did you faint?"

"When I heard your name …" I hesitated, wondering if I dared reveal my secret. The longer the papers remained at the bottom of my drawer, the more my secret weighed on me. "I heard it before, from a young man being pursued by the British."

The ivory skin of her cheeks flushed crimson, and her body tensed. "When was this?"

"That same day we met by chance. To avoid the soldier I took a shortcut through the back streets. A young man in a tasseled fez came running after me. If you recall, I had my scarf over my head, and it was almost dark. Like you, he mistook me for a Turkish woman. I could have sworn he said your name."

"You spoke to him," she said, craning forward and shifting her eyes as if to make sure no one was close by.

"I could see from his face he was frightened. The British were close behind; we even heard the click of their rifles."

"Did this young man have slanting eyes and the trace of a moustache?" She ran her fingers across her upper lip.

I nodded.

"That was Halil," said Halide with a sob. "A martyr for our cause. I have known him since he was a babe in arms."

"He gave me papers," I whispered. "I hid them in my portfolio among my drawings. By the grace of God the soldiers didn't search me."

Halide lifted her eyes and gave me a look of astonishment. "What did you do with them?"

"A man died for these papers. I felt so responsible, I kept them."

"My grandmother believed in the power of fate," said Halide. "This is surely proof of that faith. Do you realize you have the future of our struggle in your possession?"

"If they belong to your colleagues I must ..."

"I will contact you," she whispered.

We had been so engrossed in our conversation I had not noticed Connie making her way across the lawn toward the summerhouse. She was almost at the door.

"There you are," said Connie, stepping into the summerhouse. "I've been looking everywhere. Mark Bristol told me you fainted."

"Why, Mrs. Olsen, you startled me," said Halide, rising to greet her.

"You are not running a fever," said Connie, putting her palm on my forehead. "I feared you might have caught some awful disease wandering around those old neighborhoods."

"You are wise to be vigilant. Malaria is rampant, and these days the city is crowded with refugees who are in terrible health," said Halide.

"Didn't I tell you, Mary?" said Connie, giving me a triumphant look.

"That's why I prefer to stay in the country, where the air is fresh," said Halide, adjusting her veil so it covered her face once more. "Please excuse me. My husband will be wondering what has become of me."

"I have never met a Turkish woman who spoke English. Come to think of it, she is the first Turkish woman I have met since we came," said Connie after Halide left.

"Wonder where she learned to speak English so fluently?" I said, linking my arm though hers. As we walked back across the garden the moon slid from behind a cloud and cast silver shards across the waters of the Horn. The Allied battleships were bathed in an ethereal glow, like the ghosts of great sea animals risen menacingly from the deep.

# 8

Before leaving the reception, Halide had slipped her telephone number into my pocket, and I called the next day. To avoid arousing the curiosity of the consulate telephone operator, we agreed I should bring my sketchbook to her home in Rumeli Hisar near Besiktas. Two days later I set out to catch the early ferry to the village, which was on the upper reaches of the Bosphorus. I chose not to tell anyone where I was going, not even Connie. I set out early with my bag and sketching materials, affecting a casual air as if I were about to spend the morning in Beyoglu. The ferry chugged north, staying close to shore, away from the hectic traffic of ships and gondolas that skimmed like dragonflies between the Asian and European shores. We passed a bay where a graveyard swept down almost to the water, and beyond the cypresses I caught my first glimpse of the ancient castle that gave Rumeli Hisar its name. Seen from a distance, it was easy to imagine a ghostly army of Fatih, waiting, waiting in the crumbling towers for the moment to seize Byzantium.

In the shadow of the tower a French warship lay at anchor. When our ferry docked at the quay, the captain lifted his binoculars and watched the passengers as they disembarked. I hurried ashore conspicuous in my Western clothes, heedless of being seen among the milling crowd of villagers. The quay was lined with carts piled with silver fish, and the air smelled of brine. Underfoot the cobbles were slippery. Halide was waiting by the ticket office. Here in the village she wore a scarf across her hair like the local women. As we walked along the quay, people stared at my checkered dress and straw hat. We turned into a lane overhung with trees, and village clamor gave way to silence.

Their house was concealed behind an ivy-covered wall near the top of the hill. Halide led me into a space unlike any I had seen before. The walls and ceiling were paneled in dark wood. Light streamed in through a bay window and fell in parallel lines across the carpets. Colors glowed purple, blue, and green, like jewels in a dowager's necklace. Where the dye changed there were subtle variations of tone. Divans, covered with bright shawls, ran the length of three walls. Books were piled on every surface. It was there, in the dim richness of that interior, that I began to fall under the spell of the Ottomans.

An elderly woman came in, placed a tray on the table, looked at me, and then glanced at Halide. Halide poured tea into tiny glasses in filigree holders. She went through the motions of welcome, offering sticky cakes swimming in honey.

"You must forgive me if I seem distracted," she said. "Night and day I am haunted by the image of those poor people martyred on the quay at Smyrna."

She stared into her glass as if seeking the future in a crystal ball. "Why did Wilson support this outrage? Why, why, why? We had such hopes for him and his peace plan."

"I wish I knew, Halide Hanim," I replied. I had mixed feelings about the president. His moral crusade to bring peace to the world was tinged with self-righteousness. It troubled me to see how much faith Halide put in his ideals.

"This invasion was the triumph of the weak, and now I fear we are drifting toward disaster. Without Wilson's vision we have no hope of peace."

My gaze traveled over the paneled room and into the valley, where the ruins of the castle rose above the treetops. The old lady returned, carrying a dish of dried apricots; she set it on the table without looking in my direction.

"Your home is beautiful," I said, wishing to change the subject.

"Thank you," she said, nodding. "Our furnishings came from my family home; nothing here is new save for our books and our ideas."

"I have brought you some additional reading material," I said, reaching for my bag. Taking care to keep the papers in order, I placed them on the table. With a sigh close to a sob, Halide picked them up and began reading.

"You cannot imagine the value of these documents," she said. "We will be forever in your debt. If they had fallen into Allied hands our struggle would have been set back months, even years."

"It happened so fast I didn't have time to refuse the boy."

"When Halil did not come that night we feared the worst."

"Halil—was that his name?"

"We were to meet at our apartment in Pera, a small place where we live in the winter."

"I overheard the soldiers saying they had followed him from the docks."

"Maybe he tried to throw them off."

"Who was he?"

"The son of Mustafa Pasha, a legal scholar and preeminent intellectual in the Nationalist struggle. These papers represent months of work. He has laid out our Nationalist agenda within the boundaries of Ottoman law—a blueprint for the new Turkish nation."

We were interrupted by the chimes of Big Ben striking two o'clock, coming from the interior of the house.

"That clock was a wedding gift from my father. He had great admiration for the British, but now," said Halide, giving an expressive shrug, "now we do not know what to think."

The front door slammed, and Dr. Adnan strode into the room, his coat flowing behind him like a train. His eyes darted from side to side, unfocused and distracted.

"What brings you to Rumeli Hisar?" he asked.

"Don't you recall, Adnan?" Halide gave a gentle reprimand.

"It is true!" he cried. It was then his eyes lit on the documents spread across the table. Removing his glasses, he snatched up a page and held it close to his face. "They are returned to us—what a miracle. One would almost believe in a God."

"We must send word to Mustafa Pasha," said Halide.

"No need, my dear. He will be here any minute; he agreed to come with us to present our petition at Yildiz tonight."

"Now it is my turn to be forgetful," said Halide, shaking her head as she rose from the divan and walking over to the window. "Let us pray the return of his papers will help alleviate his suffering."

"I fear it will take more than that. The pasha is filled with grief and remorse for sending his son on such a mission."

"Whom else could he have trusted?" said Halide.

"I made drawings from memory," I said quietly. "The body lying in the street, the blood, his fallen fez. I had to record what I had witnessed."

"No one can see those pictures, Mary Hanim," said Adnan, suddenly serious. "The fewer people who know about this the better."

"This must be our secret; having those papers in your possession was tantamount to treason," said Halide.

Were my actions shadowed by memories of Burnham, the click of the gun, the footsteps of pursuing soldiers, the approach of sudden death? When I looked for an answer I found only darkness.

"We don't have much time," said Halide to Adnan. "Mustafa Kemal left Samsun for Amasya earlier today."

"I must telegraph Rauf at once and let him know the papers are safe."

"At dawn I will take them to Scutari."

"It is too dangerous for you to go in person. Allied spies are everywhere."

"I'll take care."

An argument ensued, and they slipped into Turkish. Leaving them to settle their differences, I wandered across that magical room and stared through the window into the garden, enclosed by an ivy-covered wall.

A wooden gate led into a lane beyond. The latch moved, the gate eased open, and a stranger stepped onto the path. He was wrapped in a cloak with its hood thrown back over his wide shoulders. Head bowed, he moved along the path with the slow step of an older man. Drawing close to the house he glanced up; on his elongated features was a look of such infinite sadness I felt a wave of compassion. How well I understood his pain

Our introduction was awkward; uncertain of what was expected, I held out my hand. The pasha bowed, grave yet polite, then turned away and walked toward the main room; at the door he hesitated, as if about to turn. His head twitched as he greeted Dr. Adnan, who was holding the manuscript in both hands. Arms outstretched, he offered it to the pasha, like a page bowing before a king.

"They appear to be in order; I haven't had time to check. We have no reason to suppose Halil kept anything."

"Mrs. Di Benedetti brought the papers this very afternoon. Halil gave them to her just before—" He broke off, his voice trembling with pain.

"I, we, owe you a great debt of thanks, ma'am," said the pasha. Like Adnan and Halide he spoke English with a slight hint of an accent.

"Not necessary," I whispered. "You do not owe me anything."

"What happened exactly?" His question was simple and direct. I was ready for it, for I had asked the same thing of the military over and over — *What happened? How did Burnham die?*

"I didn't see the shooting. My back was turned," I said quietly.

"Then tell me what went before." He stared at me, insistent.

"I was lost. I heard footsteps behind me." My voice faltered; the memory was jarring. "At that hour there wasn't a soul on the street, and at first your son frightened me. My head was covered with a shawl. It was dusk, and he obviously mistook me for a Turk."

"He gave you the papers? Just like that?"

"The British were very close. We both heard them." I was about to describe the look on Halil's face but stopped myself; there were things the father did not need to know.

"One day you will tell me, God willing," said the pasha, sensing my hesitation, "but not now. My work is only half done. I must see that these papers reach their destination — otherwise my son will have died in vain."

He looked at me and smiled. Such an unexpected expression of warmth made old feelings stir within me, emotions I thought long dead. Confused, it was my turn to look away. Propped against the opposite wall was a large poster of distinctive design; lines of Arabic script were arranged like a teardrop against an umber-colored background.

"Our resistance slogan," said Adnan, following my gaze.

"An old Turkish saying — *Buda Gecher* — which means 'This too will pass,'" said the pasha. "We Turks have infinite patience; we will wait and we will prevail."

"Our old Ottoman script is beautiful," said Halide, "and mystical. From one simple phrase the calligrapher has fashioned a work of art that describes our struggle in a pure symbolic way."

Clouds raced over the valley, obscuring the sun. The room grew dark, and a steady drumbeat of rain pounded the window.

"You must not think of taking the ferry until this has passed," said Halide.

"My sister will be worried. I didn't tell her I was coming here and she knew nothing about the papers."

"That was wise," said Halide. "They must remain our secret."

"I will make a call to Mark Bristol," said Adnan. "He is our friend, and he knows the Allies are tapping our phone."

From the bay window I watched while the storm swept in from the north. Lightning flared through the low clouds gathered above the valley, and driving rain obscured first the Bosphorus, then the castle. Finally the garden was lost behind a curtain of water. I placed my hands flat against the glass and felt the vibrations from the rain as it thudded against the window. For the first time in months I felt at peace. Perhaps it was recognition of the moment when life offers the choice of a new path and the painful past begins to wither away.

The papers had been arranged in three low piles, each weighted with a single stone. Adnan and Halide were still talking, but it was obvious that she had prevailed; I caught the words ferry and Scutari. She stroked his face when he looked annoyed. Close by, the pasha sat silent, staring into space.

Close to the time they had to leave for the palace, Halide announced I must accompany them. Day and night, agents of the sultan watched their house; it was too dangerous for me to remain alone. Halide offered to lend me the court dress that once belonged to her sister. The prospect of wearing a veil and imagining the role of a Turkish woman excited me; disguise afforded liberating anonymity.

Gradually the rain subsided, and the storm rolled away leaving the sky clear. Just after sundown we clambered into a carriage that had once belonged to Halide's grandfather. It stood high off the road on rusting springs that creaked as we got in. Inside the air was close and stale and the velvet-covered seats threadbare—worn mementoes of another era. Halide and I sat side by side, hidden behind our veils, our features impressed on the light cotton like Catholic relics. Crowded into that small space, I had to shift my knees to avoid brushing against Mustafa Pasha.

Lurching and swaying, the carriage rolled up the first hill, I stole a glance at the pasha as he stared out of the window, his profile outlined against the orange light from the carriage lamp. Poor, poor man. I wanted to reach out and touch his hand. I empathized with his suffering. He inclined his head and our eyes met. Giving him a shy smile, I looked away.

Once we reached flat ground the horses picked up their pace. As we sped along the upper road, hard springs rubbed against my lower back. I leaned forward and Halide apologized for the dilapidated state of our seats. The road turned left, and as we dragged uphill, branches from the overgrown hedgerows scratched against the windows. Suddenly we slowed, the horses whinnied, the driver cursed, and the carriage came to an abrupt stop. Adnan rolled down the window and looked out.

"English soldiers," he hissed.

We heard the crunch of boots, and a soldier thrust his head through the open window. He was ruddy faced and young, his eyes bloodshot.

"What are you doing out after dark?"

"Keep back," said Adnan. "I am a doctor. I fear my wife and sister have cholera. There is a new outbreak in our village."

Unmoved, the soldier surveyed the interior. I pressed against my seat, thankful for the anonymity afforded by my veil.

"Who's he?" the soldier asked.

"My brother-in-law. He does not speak English."

My palms were damp and my mouth felt dry with fear. What would happen if they detained us? How would I explain to John? The minutes seemed to drag by. I glanced at Halide. She put her finger to her lips and bowed her head. I did the same, praying they would let us pass.

"I'm not taking any chances with cholera," said an English voice. "Let go the reins, corporal, and stand back."

"At once, sir."

The metallic bits jangled, the driver cracked his whip, and we started forward with such a violent lurch I clutched the windowsill to stop myself from falling. The pasha's eyelids flickered and he lifted his head and gave me a smile, part reassurance, part sympathy. Beyond the window the soldiers watched from a distance.

We entered the palace grounds through a back gate guarded by a lone sentry who merely nodded as we passed. Between the trees I saw the silhouettes of buildings hunched low to the ground and the pointed roof of what seemed to be a chalet.

We passed through arched gateways into a courtyard. To our right was the dark hulk of the palace, more like a bourgeois mansion in the outskirts of Paris than a sultan's residence. A line of carriages waited by the railings.

"When I was a child my father brought me to this same courtyard to see horses the then sultan, Abdulhamid, had imported from Arabia. Beautiful creatures—so regal, with arched necks and skin as soft as silk. They were housed in specially built stables designed by a Viennese architect."

"Ah, the Ottoman obsession with all things European," said Adnan. "See where it has brought us."

We entered through the main door and found ourselves in a brightly lit hall furnished with gilded chairs and tables crammed with marble busts and unwieldy porcelain vases. An elderly man in a frock coat murmured words of welcome in stumbling French. It was clear the pasha knew where he was going; he strode ahead along a richly carpeted hall. Hindered by my veil, I struggled to keep up with him.

A pair of cream-painted doors opened onto a reception hall. Electric lightbulbs glittered in the chandeliers, giving the room a garish aspect. High in the marble-covered walls the windows were shuttered, and the hot air smelled of perspiration. At the far end on a dais stood a European-style throne, its high back and arms upholstered in red velvet. Every inch of space along the wall was occupied by courtiers and military men, their rank spelled out with lines of medals and scarlet sashes. Mustafa Pasha took a deep breath before he strode into the hall. Heads turned and eyes shifted. Some darkened with suspicion. Adnan followed, while Halide and I made our way to an area cordoned off for the women. Mustafa stood near the throne, chin jutted forward, shoulders straight, accentuating his powerful build. Who was this man, I wondered? He radiated energy. His eyes shifted, taking in everything that was going on around him.

More uniformed men bustled in and bowed to the pasha. They conversed in hushed tones with Adnan. Drums rolled, the gilded doors were flung open, and a line of soldiers marched in two by two, forming an honor guard along the length of the hall. An elderly man in a frock coat advanced toward the throne. The wire-frame glasses balanced on his broad nose shook with each step, and his fez fell low on his forehead. This, I surmised, was Mehmed VI, sultan of the former Ottoman Empire, caliph of all Islam.

The throne was so large that when the sultan sagged onto the cushions he looked like a doll tossed on a nursery chair. Scrolls were unfurled, announcements made, drumrolls played, and Dr. Adnan advanced toward the throne. He addressed the sultan in a clear and steady voice. The sultan nodded, and a stern figure in black waved Adnan away.

The doctor bowed. There was another roll of drums, and in less than fifteen minutes the ceremony ended. The four of us were ushered to the door. I paused to take one last look at the empty hall. Nothing remained of the pomp and splendor I had imagined; instead it had the bedraggled air of a ballroom emptied of dancers. Someone extinguished the light, and the great hall of the Ottomans was plunged into darkness.

When the carriage passed through the main gate the three of them broke into animated conversation, first French, then English out of deference for me.

"The sultan is a broken man," said Adnan. " I am startled by the change. How hard it was to go through the motions, knowing it will be the Allies who decide. Ah, Mary Hanim, what you see is a pale shadow of the world we once knew. For better or for worse it is finished."

# 9

When I returned to the consulate the next morning, I went at once to the admiral's office before the impressions of my visit were forgotten. I described the people and the layout of the streets. He seemed interested to hear more about the French warship and its inquisitive captain. Of Halide and Adnan I said very little save that their home was beautiful. Pressing his fingers to his chin, the admiral listened with a half smile. He liked me, I could tell. More important, he seemed to trust my observations. The visit to Yildiz, the presence of the pasha, these remained my secrets, like the papers and hidden drawings. The admiral had limits to his tolerance, and I had no desire to test them. My secrets liberated me.

Connie and John were surprisingly reticent. Apart from a few questions about Halide and her home, we talked as if I had been on an ordinary overnight trip. A wall went up between us—a barrier of silence built with experiences left unmentioned. What could I say about Mustafa or the visit to Yildiz? Such knowledge would place John in an impossible position.

A couple of days after my return, Annie Allen called the apartment.

"Halide Hanim wants the three of us to be observers at the protest meeting next week."

"Protest?" I said, staring at the phone in surprise.

"The opposition are organizing a massive demonstration against the occupation of Smyrna. Both Halide and Adnan fear the Allied authorities may cause trouble. They are enlisting impartial observers just in case."

"What have I to do with all this? Why does Halide Hanim want me there?"

"Our friend has a high regard for Americans. I assume she wants you to see for yourself how deep the feeling runs against this invasion."

"One cannot fail to notice the mood of the city has shifted."

Annie gave a sigh. "I am morally opposed to all violence; where there is suffering I see no right or wrong side."

"Halide Hanim would disagree."

"Can you come down to the admiral's office? We can discuss this later; right now we need his permission for you to leave the safety of the consulate."

Now it was my turn to sigh.

"My overriding concern is for the peace and stability of Anatolia," said Annie, leaning forward in her chair. "Christian, Muslim are all the same to me. Halide Hanim trusts my judgment; I am always impartial."

"Why did she invite Mary?" asked Mark Bristol.

"Three pairs of eyes are better than two; I will be concentrating on what is being said, Mary and Florence will observe."

"Come now, Miss Allen, that's too simplistic."

"You see ulterior motives everywhere, Admiral. It's the intelligence officer in you."

With a laugh the admiral leaned back in his chair and clasped his hands behind his head.

"I've heard they are expecting thousands."

"Knowing the Turkish people, I guarantee the meeting will be peaceful."

"It's not the Turks I'm worried about," said Admiral Bristol. "You know as well as I do the protest will be saturated with Allied spies."

"Come, sir, Allied intelligence knows all of us by now, even Mary. You can be sure a report was made the moment she set foot in Rumeli Hisar."

I listened while they bantered back and forth and wondered how long they had known one another.

"I have no objections. Mrs. Di Benedetti is free to come and go as she pleases."

"Thank you," I said. Clouds shifted, sunlight beamed into the room, and a small bald spot on the top of his head glistened.

"And I thank you," said Annie, rising to leave and indicating to me I should do the same. "It will mean a lot to Halide and Adnan; they are good friends to America."

"Will you be making a report of any sort, off the record of course?" he feigned a casual tone.

"If you wish," said Annie. "Florence Billings and I have to return to Konya by the end of the month. It will be done by then."

"I look forward to reading it," said the admiral and extended his hand. "I give you my word your observations will remain confidential."

Halide advised us to leave the car at the foot of the hill and walk to Sultanahmet Square while she went to the speakers' platform. I had never been in this part of town before. The houses were tiny, no more than two stories. Vines trailed over the ragged roofs, and geraniums, planted in old cans, brightened dark doorways. We found Mustafa Pasha waiting in the shade of an ivy-covered arch. I didn't recognize him at first, for he was wearing a dark robe over his suit. After a brief exchange with Annie Allen, he indicated we should follow him. He walked so fast we had to run to keep pace. The narrow streets were already crowded.

We followed a procession of men, some hobbling on crutches, others in uniform, medals jingling on their chests. There were working men of every age. Despite their shabby clothes they walked with heads held high. Here and there were women in *chadors* and others veiled from head to toe, all swaying toward the summit like gaggles of black geese. Arm in arm walked a cluster of younger women in short dresses and heels, light veils draped across their faces.

By the time we reached the top of the hill, the crowd filled the broad expanse of parkland in front of the mosque. I stopped, stunned by the sight of the massive domes of Haghia Sophia, apparently rising from the walls of Sultanahmet. I had never realized the two great buildings were so close that they faced each other across the square, monumental reflections of lost empires, Byzantine and Ottoman. Miss Allen caught my hand and told me not to linger. We made our way toward the square, staying close to the outer wall of Sultanahmet mosque. Overhead black flags draped from the minarets and balconies rippled in the wind. The ancient elms that surrounded the square were alive with bodies. A vast flag, black with white lettering, was draped over the railings in front of the mosque.

"It says 'Wilson's Twelfth Point,'" whispered Miss Allen. "It calls for self-determination, whatever that may mean."

"This meeting isn't just about the invasion of Smyrna," said Miss Billings.

"This is a gathering of Turkish solidarity," proclaimed Miss Allen, looking about her. "I have never seen anything like it before."

From the minarets came the cry of the muezzin; it wafted on the clear air and over the heads of the people, who gazed toward the sky.

"Allah ekber, Allah ekber," The crowd responded, chanting as one in a deep chorus, "La Ilahen, Illa Allah."

"They are chanting 'God is Great,'" said Miss Allen. "Remember that, Mary. We need every detail imprinted on our memory."

As I moved closer to Annie Allen, Mustafa Pasha and I bumped into one another. His touch filled me with unexpected desire. How can I explain the look he gave me—such melancholy and sadness—yet beneath the surface I sensed my feelings were returned.

He led us to the edge of the square, where we were met by armed soldiers who escorted the four of us to a walled courtyard where the leaders of the demonstration were gathered. To our left I noticed a flight of stone steps leading to a balcony hung with banners; this served as the speakers' platform. I caught a glimpse of Halide, somber in her chador, but she did not see me. Mustafa Pasha indicated I should stay close to his side; there were rumors Allied agents had infiltrated the enclosure.

Head lowered, Halide ascended the steps and prepared to address the crowd. Her quiet voice was transformed, possessed with the fervor of a Baptist minister.

"I am an unfortunate daughter of Islam," Miss Allen translated. "At last the European powers have found a pretext to break to pieces the Empire of the Crescent." Florence Billings and I leaned close to Miss Allen, drinking in every word. Halide's voice broke as she summoned the soul of her nation to resist partition by the Allies.

"…and these men who call the Turks sinners have sinned themselves so deeply that the great waves of the immaculate oceans cannot cleanse them.

"Governments are our enemies, the people our friends. The just revolt of our hearts is our strength."

"My goodness," murmured Miss Allen. "Halide Hanim has just crossed the line."

"Now swear and repeat with me... The sublime emotion which we cherish in our hearts will last until the proclamation of the rights of the people."

As the crowd roared her words an Allied plane dipped low, momentarily drowning the chorus. Halide left the platform, but the chanting continued.

"We must leave," hissed Miss Allen. "Adnan is concerned that once we are on the road the Allies might try to arrest the two of them."

"Won't they detain us too?" I asked.

"I am known throughout Anatolia. The Allies wouldn't dare touch me," Miss Allen replied.

A man in green robes stopped to talk with her; he bent low like a willow dipping to water.

"It's the same in the interior; Annie knows all the civic leaders, Christian and Muslim alike. Religious differences mean nothing to her," Florence Billings whispered.

We crossed the speakers' enclosure and found Adnan and Halide near the gate.

"We cannot stay here," said Adnan. "After this Halide Hanim will be at the top of their wanted list."

"You go with them. I'll find our driver," said Miss Billings. "If I can drive field ambulances across battlefields, I can help him negotiate Istanbul's back streets."

Halide pulled her veil over her face, Annie Allen took her arm, and we followed Adnan. Miss Billings walked ahead, her improbable floral hat bobbing above the heads of the crowd. As we left the enclosure, the pasha remained close to my side.

A group of clean-shaven men, each wearing a scarlet fez, was clustered in the shadow of the Egyptian monument, reading the Koran. It wasn't until we were almost level with them that I caught the eye of the youngest. If it hadn't been for the fez I could have sworn it was Private Tompkins. In the fateful seconds I hesitated to take a second look, I became separated from the others. Bewildered, I scanned the faces of the crowd thronging close to me, praying Mustafa would turn back to find me. Someone tapped my shoulder and whispered my name. I turned to find myself face to face with a stranger. Drops of perspiration, dyed red from his fez, ran down his cheeks and over his crisp white collar.

"So here you are all alone," he whispered, moving close. I felt his breath on my cheek.

"Who are you?" I said. My mouth felt dry.

"Parks, Sergeant Barnaby Parks at your service."

"What are you doing here?"

"Thought I was in jail, did you? Out of the way, all thanks to your Admiral Bristol. I told my HQ; told 'em, straight, I was just doing my duty."

"You killed a man," I said, clenching my fists to stop trembling.

"A bloody Turk."

"An unarmed man, lying wounded in the street."

"My brother was slaughtered by those bastards," he said, so close now I could smell the perspiration on his body. "Picked off like a duck on a pond. He didn't stand a chance."

People thronged around us but no one gave us a second look; in the midst the crowd I was alone with my tormentor.

"Gallipoli, Gallipoli—the name haunts me," he went on in a voice hoarse with anger. "A bloodbath, a slaughter, worse than anything in the trenches. Poor Thomas Parks died there; nineteen, nineteen years old."

This all happened so quickly I didn't have time to react. I walked on without looking back for fear of catching his eye.

"I was there too; saw the slaughter. Bodies stacked ten deep in the sea. Me and my mates we had to walk over them, like a bloody bridge of corpses. Are you listening to me?"

Spittle fell on the back of my neck; I started with fright but dared not turn around.

"Rotting, decaying, worms crawling through their guts, flesh falling off the bones; the stench of hell. My God, that smell," he went on, spurred by my fear. "They put the head of an Aussie on a rock, his hat on his skull, poor bastard's mouth open like he seen the devil 'imself, and his corpse picked over by birds, sinews hangin' out of his neck like the Sunday joint."

Desperation grew in my chest and my gorge rose while the crowds surged around us, oblivious to my terror.

"You rich scum sit safe at 'ome while kids like my brother Thomas do the dying. Now people like you make the Turks their friends." Terrified, I looked around for Halide and Mustafa, but the crowd had swallowed them up. I broke into a run; people muttered as I pushed past, but still he kept close behind me. His fez tumbled to the ground, revealing his true identity.

"Got my gun right here. One shot, behind the ear, bang, clean into the brain. No court of law will put me away for shootin' a traitor."

At the mention of a weapon I was struck with a wave of fear so strong I thought I might faint. As we reached the outer rim of the hippodrome, the crowd thinned, and stragglers lay resting on the skimpy grass. Ahead I saw a low wall running between the plaza and a half-ruined palace decorated with glistening tile. Annie Allen was standing on a stone ledge shading her eyes against the sun; I thought I would collapse with relief.

"Mary, Mary, we've been looking..." Her voice faded as she took in the sergeant, pistol in hand, trailing close behind me. At the sound of her voice he slipped his arm around my neck and pulled me to his chest in a chokehold. He was strong; under his coat his muscles were taut. Closing my eyes I saw Connie, the streets of New York, Burnham walking on the beach in Provincetown—all flashed before me in a second.

Parks tightened his grip as Annie stepped down onto the dirt and started walking toward him, arms outstretched.

"You are a brave man," she said quietly. "You fought a terrible war. Don't do anything foolish now it is all over."

"Stay back," he hissed.

My eyes met Annie's; she did not blink. I was too numb to do anything.

"Drop your gun," she said firmly. "There are people everywhere; you cannot get away."

"Bloody Turk-lovers. I hate…"

He screamed, and his grip relaxed. Without thinking I ran toward Annie and collapsed sobbing in her arms. Looking back I saw Mustafa Pasha wrestling the sergeant to the ground. Within seconds a dozen onlookers had pounced on his legs and torso; someone tossed the gun toward the foot of the wall. The last thing I heard was Parks cursing Mustafa as Annie led me away to the car waiting in a back street near the Hippodrome.

# 10

Summer was approaching, and the city sweltered under a heat wave. Even though the long windows were thrown open and the electric fans were turned to full power, the rooms in the consulate became hot and stuffy. Sleep became difficult. I tossed and turned, haunted by images of the leering sergeant and the smell of his stale breath close to my neck. As the night hours passed I was nagged by the sense that certainty had vanished; life was ever changing and unpredictable.

Consulate life slowed as the staff got ready to move to the summer consulate, which was housed in a wooden mansion in a waterside village a mile or two up the Bosphorus beyond Rumeli Hisar. Even though I welcomed the thought of fresh air and cool breezes, I didn't want to lose contact with Halide and Mustafa. They stimulated me. The world she inhabited influenced my vision, giving it new direction and meaning. Now the sergeant was behind bars, and the lost manuscript was safe in the hands of Halide's colleagues. I wondered if our growing friendship would fade. Little did I know everything was about to take another unexpected turn.

The encounter with the sergeant had left me feeling shaken. I had never been physically assaulted before. No matter how strong I fancied my will, in the face of brute force I had been powerless, at the mercy of a madman. For days afterward I remained inside the solid walls of the consulate, where I retreated to my studio to finish a series of drawings of Eyoub Camii. According to Halide, this was the most sacred mosque in the city. It housed the remains of Eyoub Ensari, standard-bearer and friend of the Prophet, killed defending the banner during a siege against the Byzantines. The lines of these drawings were delicate and shaded with the lightest wash of sepia-toned watercolor, quite different from my bold and vivid oils.

It must have been late June, probably a week or so after the meeting in Sultanahmet Square. I had finished painting for the day and was seated at the table going over my section of the report Annie was preparing for Admiral Bristol. Annie urged me to give a detailed account of the incident with the sergeant, not only for the admiral, but also for the British authorities who were pressing charges for murder and assault. Recounting what had happened wasn't easy. I sat sucking my pen, at a loss for words.

A light tap at the door disturbed me. The handle turned, and Miss Harrison, John's secretary, stood on the threshold clutching an envelope in her left hand. Light-skinned and delicate, she was transparent, like gauze. Her face registered unease.

"This came for you by messenger; he's waiting downstairs for a response."

"Who's writing to me?"

"Halide Hanim."

I tore the envelope open. Two cards were inside. One was in Arabic script, the other in English from Halide explaining that Latife Hanim, Mustafa's mother, was inviting me to their home on Tuesday afternoon. Intrigued, I turned the letter over and tried to make out the signature—of course, none of it made any sense. My desire troubled me. I hardly knew this man. The murdered boy had a mother, and wherever she might be, she was suffering. I had to keep a distance.

Miss Harrison coughed and reminded me an immediate response was needed. Without a second thought I scrawled a note of acceptance; what harm would there be in a visit to an elderly woman in her own home? The outing promised to be another adventure; now that the sergeant was imprisoned I was safe, and besides, Halide had promised to come with me and translate.

I was still puzzling over the invitation when there was another knock. Before I could respond, the door swung open. Mark Bristol stood on the threshold. Light fell on his face, and I noticed the creases in his brow had deepened.

"Good, you are alone," he said, closing the door behind him. "We have a serious matter to discuss."

I laid the pad on my lap; the solemn edge in his voice demanded my full attention.

"A rare privilege has been extended to you," he said.

I wasn't sure I understood him, so I smiled.

"You accepted, of course, without asking. I knew you would."

"You know about the invitation?" I asked.

"I am aware of everything that goes on in my consulate. Your safety is my responsibility, Mary."

"So you came to tell me I must refuse."

"On the contrary." He gave me a direct look. "This lady has lost her grandson; you must offer your condolences. After all, you were the last to see him alive."

"Except for the murderer." I felt my cheeks flushing. To hide my confusion I stared at the floor.

"Halide Hanim will take care of you," he said, wrapping his hand around the doorknob. "She is a friend to America, so you will be in good hands. But remember, the Allies will be watching the house. My powers of intervention are limited."

The drone of the muezzin began, twining its way over the rooftops and seeping into the consulate garden so even the street dogs lounging beside the main gate began to howl. The admiral smiled, touched his forehead in a half salute, and disappeared into John's office. Little did I know the situation was about to become more complicated.

The following afternoon was bright. Halide came on the dot of three. It took more than an hour to reach Arnvutkoy, one of the fishing villages scattered along the banks of the Bosphorus. Halide and I were shown to a grand living room so close to the water I felt I was floating midstream. Reflections from the water dappled the walls a shimmering silver and blue as a passing ferry disturbed the flow. This then was his childhood home, I thought, taking in the ornate grandeur: marble-topped tables, gilded sofas, even a grand piano; rich carpets woven in silk and a divan covered in paisley shawls.

We rose as a small figure dressed in black came toward us, dignified like a grand duchess; the resemblance to her late grandson took me by surprise. There was the same nose, the same aquiline features, but weathered by age. Behind her came a procession of maids carrying a samovar, trays, china, and sweetmeats. Halide rose and kissed her hand. They exchanged a formal greeting. Latife Hanim Efendi clapped her hands and tea was served in china cups, European style.

"So you are Mrs. Di Benedetti." Her demeanor was grave. "Welcome to my home. My son has told me of your great courage."

I wanted to protest but feared doing so lest it trivialize her loss. I smiled and gave a slight bow. Latife Hanim intrigued me. On each cheek was a careful circle of rouge, and her eyes were rimmed with kohl. When she wasn't talking, she was assessing us, with the same searing expression her son used.

Beyond the window I heard the drone of an engine. An Allied warship chugged downstream, rattling the windows and sending waves lashing against the side of the house. Lined up on deck, sailors in white uniforms stood stiff. A British flag fluttered from the bow.

"A generation of our finest youth was sacrificed so this would not come to pass," said Latife Hanim. "I praise God my beloved husband is not alive to witness our humiliation."

Suddenly one of the side doors swung open and a dark-haired girl perhaps eight or nine years old danced into the room. She bore a startling resemblance to Mustafa.

"Who is that?" I whispered.

"Nilufer, the daughter of Zeynep Hanim, Mustafa's elder sister," Halide explained.

I relaxed, but my reprieve was short lived. Close behind the girl came a strange contraption resembling an oversized wheelbarrow, pushed by a sturdy maid. I remember noticing how her red hands clutched the handles tightly. She steered with a determined look on her face. The barrow was piled high with silk-covered pillows. I didn't see the wraithlike figure at first. She was wrapped in a woolen shawl and almost hidden by the billowing cushions. With painful slowness the maid navigated her way through the maze of furnishings and set the barrow down beside Latife Hanim. Pillows were plumped and the ailing woman was pulled upright so she was half lying and half sitting. Like Latife Hanim, she was clad in somber black.

"May I present Gul Hanim. She has been eager to meet you, our honored guest," said the old lady. With slow, tender movements she ran her hand across the invalid's face.

I knew at once this was Mustafa's wife and was filled with pity. Halide murmured something in Turkish and moved to embrace her. I watched as Gul Hanim's frail arms wove around Halide's neck and stroked her hair.

"Gul and I have known each other since childhood," said Halide, returning to her chair. "She has been living in her father's house in Sariyer. After Halil's death she returned here to share the burden of her loss with Latife Hanim."

"Please tell them I can only imagine the depth of their grief," I said.

"I am old, I have suffered many losses, but this was the worst," said Latife Hanim.

As we sipped our tea in silence, the minutes passed slowly. Time shifts after the death of a loved one; its passage is relentless like the steady drip of water that builds an iceberg.

Waves crashed against the side of the house, and the boom of a ship's horn echoed from the straits. Nilufer glanced up, set her teacup on a side table and ran to window. I remember noticing how her heavy braid swung across her back. She climbed onto a chair and pressed her face and hands against the glass. Latife Hanim's mouth compressed into a thin line. She frowned and clapped her hands. At once Nilufer returned to her side, where she sat demurely, her hands folded on her lap.

"Would you like Turkish tea or European style?" Halide translated while the old lady returned to the business in hand.

"Why Turkish, of course," I replied, trying not to look at the invalid.

Finger sandwiches were passed, then cakes, French style with pink icing and cream; apart from the strong black tea, nothing Turkish was served.

Gul Hanim raised her thin and claw-like hand, bent at the knuckles as if disfigured by arthritis. Latife leaned toward her and listened while the sick woman gasped into her ear.

"Gul Hanim was anxious to meet you, Mrs. Di Benedetti," said Latife, sitting upright again. "Your bravery saved Mustafa's work from falling into Allied hands and gave meaning to Halil's terrible death. Gul Hanim adored Halil; his breath was her breath. You will forever be in her prayers."

"Please don't thank me. I did what anyone would have done under the circumstances. The soldiers were closing in on him."

"One day you must tell us more of what happened, but not now," said Latife Hanim.

Gul Hanim's brooding eyes rested on me; they were dark, dramatized by layers of kohl and dark circles that reached her cheeks. Then her mind shifted. Fire entered her gaze, and I sensed between us a strange connection.

Latife Hanim walked outside with us to the carriage, where the air was weighted with the smell of jasmine. At the foot of the carriage steps she took my hand, lifted her face toward me, and whispered, "Adieu." As we clattered down the street I looked back at the house. In one of the upper rooms the blinds shifted, and the silhouette of a figure in shawls appeared behind the window as the sun went behind a cloud.

"I have not seen Gul Hanim for many years. Her appearance was a shock," said Halide, sinking back into her seat.

"Halil was her son?" I said, not daring to acknowledge her relationship to Mustafa.

Halide nodded. "Once upon a time Gul Hanim was a vivacious, pretty woman. Now I fear she is not long for this world."

"What a tragedy for Mustafa Pasha."

"He has buried himself in his work, but he is wise enough to know he cannot escape from his pain. His son meant the world to him."

We had taken the back road through the hills. I had been so absorbed in my thoughts I scarcely notice we had reached the outskirts of a village. Halide leaned out and asked the driver to stop close to an ivy-covered wall broken by pair of wrought iron gates hanging on rusty hinges. Beyond, a drive lined with plane trees curved toward a wooden mansion half hidden by the trees. Pale light filtered through the foliage, casting long shadows across the façade.

"My childhood home," said Halide. "That was the *selamlik*; unfortunately we cannot see the *harem* from the road; it is farther down the hill."

"You mean there really is such a thing as a harem?"

"It's the women's quarters," she said with a laugh. "An Arab word. I was born in the harem, in the same room as my mother and her mother before her. Once upon a time we felt safe within those old walls; I fear we dwelt in illusion."

"I'd like to see where you were born," I said, reaching for the door handle.

Halide leaned forward and put her hand on mine. "We cannot enter. The French commandeered this house for one of their generals."

"Surely you have a right to visit."

"I am a Muslim; I have no rights."

"It was your home."

"I was twelve when my grandfather died and Granny moved the household to the Asian shore," she sighed. "We heard that the family who was living here was tossed out like old furniture. Even the servants who had been with us for generations were left to fend for themselves."

A soldier slouched from the main door and kicked the ground with the toe of his boot, scattering stones into the bushes. Shouldering his rifle, he started toward the gate. Halide drew back behind the curtain and tapped the roof of the carriage; the driver cracked his whip, and we moved on.

"I wonder what will become of this place," she said softly. "No one can afford to live this way any more; the old way of life is dying."

The wall gave way to an orchard bounded by gently arching plane trees. We passed luxuriant gardens, a blur of white, violet and pink, and then more houses, half hidden behind walls heavy with wild roses and wisteria, shuttered, silent, slumbering in the afternoon sun.

Two days later British Headquarters informed Admiral Bristol that Sergeant Parks had escaped from custody. Parks left a note in his cell threatening revenge on everyone responsible for putting him behind bars.

# 11

At the end of June the peace treaty was signed in the Great Hall of Mirrors at the Palace of Versailles, just outside Paris. Hundreds gathered to witness the signing ceremony; the pact with Germany was sealed, and an uneasy peace descended on Europe. The world leaders then quit Paris for their own capitals, leaving behind a staff of commissioners to consolidate the loose ends. Wilson returned to Washington, where he faced a battle with Congress and the Senate to ratify the terms of the treaty.

A sense of unease lingered at the consulate, and the fate of the Ottoman territories remained unresolved. Despite a last-minute plea delivered in person by Damad Ferid, the Turkish prime minister, France, Italy, Greece, and Great Britain were obdurate in their refusal to leave the Ottoman Empire intact. Each country coveted a share of the spoils promised in the wartime treaties; these competing territorial claims often overlapped, and one claim was pitted against another.

The discomfort was compounded by reports from Anatolia about the activities of Mustafa Kemal, who was reorganizing the disparate factions of the disbanded Ottoman army into a cohesive fighting force. Kemal, like most Turks, was bitterly opposed to the occupation. Slowly, rumors of their growing strength filtered back to Istanbul, making the Allies and the government uneasy.

At the end of June, on the same day the treaty was signed, Sergeant Parks was seen lingering outside the gates of the summer consulate in Tarabya disguised as a local man. The guards gave chase, but he disappeared into the back streets. This news came just as my belongings were packed and I was about to join Connie and John in Tarabya. Admiral Bristol happened to be in Istanbul for a few days on leave from the Smyrna Commission. He called the apartment and advised me to remain in the city until other arrangements had been made. As I replaced the receiver, the hollow feeling in my stomach gave way to a moment of fear. Obsessed, Parks was still stalking me; he would not give up until one of us was dead.

Several hours later the admiral sent me a note; Halide and Adnan had invited me to spend the summer with them in Rumeli Hisar. I whooped with joy at the prospect of returning to the peaceful old-world atmosphere of their home.

I was given a room in what had once been the harem; it was light filled and airy, with a high ceiling and whitewashed walls. Furnishings were spare, in the manner of the Ottomans. Along one wall was a divan covered in turquoise silk, and in the corner was a painted cupboard where the blankets were stored. I raised the blind and looked out. Directly below my window was the vegetable garden enclosed by a crumbling wall. Beyond lay a forested valley where a mist hovered above the treetops, softening the outline of the hills.

"You will be comfortable here," said Halide, "and more protected than you would be in Tarabya, where there are many foreigners these days. In our village everyone knows everyone else. A stranger would be noticed at once."

"You didn't mind my coming here at the last minute? It is generous of you, Halide."

"It was the admiral's idea," she said, "and to be honest, Adnan and I had reservations at first. I didn't know if you would be comfortable with all the coming and going. You have become a good friend, Mary, and sympathetic to our cause."

Halide stood framed in the door. While she was talking, a spindly boy with wild, dark eyes sidled up to her and slipped his arm around her waist.

"Well, who is this?" I asked.

"Ali Ayetullah, my younger son from my first marriage."

The boy shifted from one foot to the other and stared at me with ill-concealed curiosity.

"He has your eyes," I said, trying to conceal my astonishment; Halide had never spoken of her children before. "How old are you, Ali Ayetullah?"

The boy turned away from my extended hand and stared at the floor.

"Don't be foolish," said Halide, pushing him forward.

"I am thirteen ma'am," he replied, giving me a limp handshake.

"Ali and his brother Hassan are students at Robert College; Ali has been ill, so he has been living at home for a while, but he must return next week."

"I won't go back." Ali wrenched his hand away from mine and glared at Halide.

"You are almost a man; a man cannot remain at home with his mother," said Halide. "Go downstairs and finish your homework. I fear you will fall behind your classmates."

"I don't care, I'm not going."

"Your behavior shames me in front of our guest."

Giving one last glowering look at Halide, Ali walked across the hall and clattered down the stairs.

"It is easier to plan a revolution than be a mother," sighed Halide once her son had gone.

"I didn't know you had children," I said, picking up the boxes of charcoal and arranging them in a line on the windowsill—trying to distract myself from that familiar sadness I felt when the subject of children was raised.

"The boys are my life, but as our struggle intensifies, I am trying to detach myself from sentimental ties." She sighed. "But it is hard, very hard."

"A high price to pay," I replied.

"If I don't dedicate myself to our cause like my male colleagues, my sons will have no future in this country."

A surge of wind blew a branch of wisteria against the window; it scratched against the glass. Along the garden wall the cypresses swayed.

"A storm is brewing," said Halide. "I must instruct the maids to shutter the windows. Make yourself comfortable. Nakie Hanim will ring the bell for dinner. We eat early so our colleagues can get home before dark."

# 12

Sightings of Sergeant Parks continued, then suddenly silence, as if the city had swallowed him up. After a while I stopped thinking about him. The interior walls of the house were thick, and my room was silent save for birdsong from the trees outside my window and the distant drone of the muezzin. Every morning I worked alone and undisturbed, watching the light shift as the sun climbed higher.

In the late afternoons, I took long walks across the hills and into the wooded valley below the castle. Halide and Adnan insisted I be accompanied by one of the groundskeepers and his dog. They kept a respectful distance and did not interrupt when I stopped to make quick drawings of the landscape — simple impressions of light and texture rather than photographic reproductions. My relation to my surroundings shifted. The invisible threads that bound me to the trees, hills, and the earth itself grew stronger, more intense. I worked with pastels, blending color upon color to capture the tone and quality of the light. My figures shrank to mere specks, dwarfed by nature. My interest shifted to the dynamic tension between the inner and outer world.

I remember it was July 10, Burnham's birthday, when Halide and Adnan received a coded message from Erzerum. It was two or three days before the Ottoman government ordered Mustafa Kemal to return to Istanbul. Rather than disobey the sultan, Major Kemal, the war hero and loyal soldier devoted to the military, resigned from the army. The government then ordered the commander of the Eastern forces, Kiazim Kara Bekir Pasha, to arrest Kemal for disobeying the sultan. Kiazim Pasha refused. Now that Mustafa Kemal had broken completely from Istanbul, he assumed the leadership of the Nationalist movement. The stage was set for the next act.

That same night we gathered in the main room, ten of us all seated around a low table covered with dishes of eggplant cooked with tomato, rice, lamb, vegetables in olive oil, and fresh beans. I remember that meal because Mustafa Pasha was there; my heart leaped when I saw him.

"So you are one of us now," he said, "with the blessing of Admiral Bristol." It was the first time we had spoken since my visit to his mother's house. I had many questions but felt constrained.

He had dressed formally for dinner in a Western-style tailored suit, white shirt, and navy tie knotted high at his throat. His beard was trimmed, his hair short beneath his tasseled fez.

"Mary has the soul of an Ottoman," said Halide. "Our home has calmed her spirit and helped her work."

"You are blessed to have such a gift," said Mustafa. "In my youth I dreamed of dedicating my life to painting."

"You are a man of secrets," exclaimed Halide. *How true*, I reflected.

"That was thirty years ago, during my student days at the Sorbonne. I numbered artists among my friends. The freedom of their life appealed to me."

"It is our good fortune you chose law over art," said Adnan.

"My father sent me to Paris to study politics; it was my duty to follow his wishes. I could not disappoint him."

"That's why you are fluent in French," I said.

"I learned French as a boy here in Istanbul." He smiled at me. "In Paris I learned about democracy and its application through the rule of law."

"Halide told me you are to address the conference on this subject," said Adnan.

"There will be a vote on my outline," said Mustafa. "I will be there to defend it if there are detractors. Fortunately my ideas have the support of Mustafa Kemal."

"You have a long journey ahead of you," said Adnan, looking up from his plate. "When will you be leaving us?"

"The day after tomorrow, God willing."

"So soon?" I exclaimed, feeling as if an icy wind had blown into the room.

"Erzerum is two weeks' journey from here," said Halide, giving me a querying look.

"The time has come for me to join our colleagues in Anatolia," said Mustafa Pasha. "After the death of my son I stayed for my mother's sake, and for Halil's mother, but I cannot remain here any longer."

"They will miss you," I murmured, struggling to conceal my emotions.

"My mother understands that our revolution demands total commitment; she will take care of Gul Hanim."

His gaze rested on my face and tears welled in his eyes—or was it my imagination stirred by the flickering candlelight?

"Let's drink to our struggle," he said, reaching for a glass of raki.

Everyone at the table raised their glasses; I lifted my arm as if in a trance. My body felt disconnected from my brain. He was leaving, and I might never see him again. When he turned away, I stole surreptitious glances at his profile and held fast to the memory, for I knew I would think about him every day.

That night I dreamed that Burnham had disintegrated; nothing remained save a pile of ash. I woke with a start and imagined he was sitting at the end of the bed watching me through those hooded eyes of his, like a bird of prey. Sleep was impossible. I wrapped myself in a shawl and sat by the window, staring out over the darkened hills. Something moved near the back gate; a shadow flickered and vanished. I peered into pitch darkness, my mouth dry from fear. Suddenly the glow from a lighted cigarette outlined the profile of a man moving slowly along the path beside the back wall.

Pulling on my robe, I tiptoed into the darkened hallway and felt my way along the wall with my hands. My knee struck the corner of a side table, and it fell against the hard floor with a crash.

"*Kim var?*" It was Adnan's voice, sounding alarmed.

"It's me, Adnan. There's someone in the garden."

I heard the shuffling sound of footsteps, the door handle clicked, and Adnan stood before me in his nightshirt, an oil lamp in his hand.

"An intruder—are you certain?"

"He was smoking a cigarette. I saw the glow by the wall next to the old kitchen."

"Let me rouse the gardeners; we will investigate."

"Take the shotgun," said Halide. "It's in the tack room by the back door." She followed him into the hall still in her nightgown. Her hair stuck out around her head in a wild mass of curls. The intimacy of our encounter made me feel awkward. I wasn't used to seeing them this way.

"Whatever you do, stay inside, Halide—no heroics," said Adnan.

"Come," she said taking my arm, "let's go downstairs. I'll make coffee. At this time of year the maids usually leave a small fire burning low in the small grate."

We made our way to the kitchen, a square room with whitewashed walls and a flagstone floor, dominated by a wooden table polished to a sheen. I had never been there before; during the day it was the province of Nakie Hanim and the servants.

"Did you see them?"

"It was too dark—he was by the wall."

"Just one man?"

"I think so," I said.

"They must have been watching the house. Our watchdog died a couple of days ago, and Nakie Hanim swears the poor beast was poisoned." Halide moved around the room pulling open cupboards, setting out cups, moving the coffee pot to and from the burner to the counter. She was always so resolute, and it was startling to see that she was nervous.

"Praise God you saw him. I shudder to think what might have happened."

"I was woken by a bad dream."

"Your dream was our blessing," said Halide, still pacing between the grate and the table.

"Do you think it might have been Parks?" I said. "A few weeks ago he was seen near the summer consulate."

"I suspect a local—someone who knew that back road."

Before I could respond, Adnan strode into the kitchen wiping the dirt from his hands against his nightshirt.

"He ran off toward the hills."

"Did you recognize him?" said Halide.

"Too dark." Adnan shook his head. "This was no ordinary intruder; look what Ahmet found on the path." Adnan reached into the pocket of his nightshirt and held up a metal rod, flattened at one end.

"Let me see, my dear," said Halide, taking the rod from her husband and peering at it closely. "This is a professional tool — a jimmy I think it is called. Look there, an inscription says 'Made in Sheffield.'"

"Our enemies are growing bolder," said Adnan, sinking onto a chair. "Now that Mustafa Kemal is organizing our forces, this government and the Allies are frightened; they will stop at nothing."

# 13

Halide worked for the Red Crescent, the Turkish equivalent of the Red Cross, and stored clothing and blankets she had collected for the refugees from the Balkans and Anatolia. Every Thursday she made the long journey from Rumeli Hisar to the mosque of Eyoub, where she helped to run a soup kitchen. Mosques were more than places of worship; within their confines were schools, libraries, and hospitals for the sick and dying. I had even heard of a lunatic asylum in a mosque near Edirne, where the inmates had been treated with music therapy since the time of Suleiman the Magnificent.

I joined her on the Thursday after Mustafa left for the East. I rose before dawn, woken by the first call to prayer. We left the house while it was still dark. Guided by a gardener carrying a lamp, we made our way through the village to the quay, which was crowded with workmen and women on their way to market. We bought *simit* from the bakery near the quay and tea from a vendor on the ferry. Sitting on deck, I watched the sun rise above the Asian Hills; the sky turned pink, then lavender, and the Bosphorus gleamed like liquid mercury. I felt a deep peace I had not known for a long time.

By the time we reached the docks at Galata the sun was high and the waters of the Horn were jammed with ferries, fishing boats, caiques, and battleships. Gulls wheeled screaming into the wind, and the air was filled with the clamor of ships' horns and clanging trams. We transferred to a puffball of a boat, the Eyoub ferry, and left the quay in a cloud of belching steam. Halide fell silent and gazed at the Allied warships that towered above us like sheer cliffs of iron. The captain, a wiry man with strong limbs, spat into the water. Passing close to the *Scorpion*, Admiral Mark Bristol's flagship, I overheard snatches of conversation drifting from the deck. It jarred me to hear American voices again, like an echo of a home thoroughly foreign to me now.

I knew that Admiral Bristol was still in Smyrna. The invading army had maintained its hold on the port city, and Greeks, confident of victory, walked through the streets of Istanbul shoving aside Turks. Blue-and-white flags fluttered, in premature triumph, from every Greek home, and a portrait of the Greek prime minister, Venizelos, hung from the outer wall of the Patriarch's palace in Phanar. Rumors whirled through the city. Some said Byzantium would be restored to its former glory; others claimed the Russians and the British were squabbling over its division. All agreed the fate of the Turks would soon be settled by someone other than themselves.

By the time we reached Eyoub it was almost ten o'clock; hot air rose from the cobblestones and shimmered like a mirage. Someone warned Halide they had seen a British patrol in the village earlier that morning, so we took a circuitous route through the back streets, where the smell of horse manure, urine, and sweat was almost unbearable.

I was not prepared for the sheer numbers of people waiting to be fed. There were men on crutches, some without limbs, others bandaged with grimy rags, and women with babies in their arms. There were healthy-bodied men who looked away when we passed as if shamed by their plight. It was the elderly who were the saddest—bent, gray, leaning on sticks, some even sleeping in the shadow of the walls. Children were everywhere, scampering through the streets and in and out of the vast cemetery that covered the hills above Eyoub.

"They are tempting the wrath of the *peris*," said Halide, stopping to watch a group of girls hiding among the fallen gravestones.

"Didn't you tell me the supernatural forces had vanished since the foreign armies came?" I tried to recall a conversation we had had about her grandmother, who, she claimed, had been able to see spirits.

"Eyoub is a holy place, where the power of the peris is potent," Halide explained in matter-of-fact tones, as one might talk of a long lost cousin. "These days children have no knowledge of these things."

We turned into a dusty road bordered by high walls that enclosed the mosque and the tomb of Eyoub. As we pushed our way through the crowd, heads turned and hundreds of pairs of eyes watched as we made our way toward an arched gateway halfway down the street.

"We're here, now where's the key?" said Halide, searching her cloak pocket.

"Do you have enough food?" I glanced over my shoulder. The refugees kept their distance, watching intently while Halide turned the key in the lock. Hinges creaked and the gates swung open. Gripping her arm, I followed her inside. We entered an enclosed yard shaded by giant plane trees and surrounded on three sides by arched cloisters. At the far end of the yard were rows of trestle tables sagging under tureens of hot beans and rice. Workers from the local branch of the Red Crescent had been cooking since dawn. About a dozen people were waiting behind the tables. Behind me I heard shuffling and rustling as the crowd surged after us. I dared not look around — one false step and I would be trampled.

Someone handed me a ladle and gestured toward the table. Somehow the horde had rearranged itself into a line, and the old and sick had been pushed to the front.

At a signal from Halide they swelled toward the table. I spent the rest of the day ladling food until my back ached and my feet were sore from standing in one place. The never-ending procession of tired faces began to blur, one into another. All day Halide moved between the kitchen and the courtyard issuing orders with crisp authority. Sometimes her eyes above her veil looked anxious. The pathetic condition of the people disturbed her.

She had confessed to me earlier that she wondered if she had the strength to continue the interminable fight for independence. Her physical health was fragile. She was subject to headaches and fits of fainting—only her "inner smile" sustained her. Though her struggle, and the people's, had been long, first against the autocracy of Sultan Abdul Hamid and then against the Young Turk rulers who had overthrown him, Halide had faith in her people. She confessed that sometimes her resolve wavered when the problems seemed so vast and insurmountable.

"We must gain the trust of the people. Unless we teach these masses the meaning of democracy, our efforts will only skim the surface," she told me. "When I see the numbers, I understand it will be a lifelong task."

The low light of evening began to descend, the crowds thinned, and we started clearing the tureens and moving the tables back to the kitchen. Suddenly some boys playing near the gate cried out, and a hush descended on the courtyard. I looked up and saw two soldiers framed in the archway. Shouldering their rifles, they marched across the grass, sending waves of fear among the few refugees who were left in the courtyard. Stopping a couple of feet away from my table, the soldiers stared around. To my horror, I realized one of them was Private Tompkins. Was I fated to be forever haunted by that night?

"What do you want?" asked Halide, who was standing close by.

"You speak English?" said Tompkins, his voice filled with suspicion.

"As well as you do."

"We have orders to search this place," said Tompkins.

"Are you aware that this is sacred ground?" Halide asked.

"Don't give us trouble, ma'am."

"Eyoub is the holiest mosque in the city and out of bounds to the Allies," she said in a firm voice. All eyes were on her as she moved around the table and held out her arm as if showing them to the door.

"We have reason to believe there are arms concealed here," said Tompkins. His voice quavered.

"Have you a warrant?"

"Just a routine check."

"If the authorities learn you have violated holy ground without a warrant, there will be a high price to pay."

How I admired her; she was bluffing, but her confidence gave her authority, and Tompkins was a man accustomed to taking orders. He shouldered his rifle and gave her a shrewd, assessing look. I held my breath, praying he would not notice me. As he passed, his gaze shifted, and a flicker of recognition registered in his pale eyes. We watched as the soldiers marched back across the yard and disappeared toward the town.

"That was close," said Halide. Picking up an empty tureen, she began hauling it toward the kitchen.

"I think he recognized me," I said, heaving a pot from the table.

"You are well known to the Allied authorities," said Halide with a laugh. "Come, I have something to show you."

I followed her into the ancient kitchen, which was dark with age. Generations of soot blackened the cavernous ceiling and walls. A massive fireplace occupied an entire wall. Now the embers were low, and dying coals glowed red in the grate. Following Halide's example, I placed the tureen on a slatted shelf close to a vat of soapy water where workers were washing the day's utensils.

Taking my arm, Halide led me across the kitchen. From the depths of the pile she withdrew a metal pipe. Looking closer, I recognized the barrel of a rifle.

"So there *are* weapons," I said.

"For the Nationalist army; piece by piece we smuggle them to the interior."

"Why are you showing me?"

"You are my friend. I want to be honest with you. Don't harbor any illusions about the seriousness of what we are doing," she said. She thrust the rifle toward me. I had a terrifying sense of power as I fingered the trigger. How easy, in the blink of an eye, to be master over life and death. My head reeled and I stumbled sideways. Halide grabbed the rifle and held it to her breast as one would cradle a child.

# 14

It was about this time I first heard the name Robert Dunn. As I recall, I was visiting Connie and John at the summer consulate in Tarabya one drowsy afternoon in the late summer. Overcome by heat, my sister and I were slouched in deck chairs, shaded by a massive beech tree. John sat on the steps to the house, a straw hat tilted over his forehead. The Bosphorus stretched away before us, buzzing with caiques—slender boats carrying clusters of veiled ladies, poled by boatmen with powerful arms. Suddenly the peace was shattered by a siren, and I peered into the distance where the blue hills opened toward the Black Sea. A strange craft, flat and square like a ocean liner with the top sliced off, moved downstream at a great speed, rocking the caiques and showering the consulate dock with foamy spray.

"What on earth...?"

"The weekly ferry from Trabzon," murmured Connie, her eyes still closed. "It's always packed with Russian refugees. I feel so sorry for them."

"The pilot must be drunk," I said, watching the craft weave among the small boats. "Look at the speed he is moving; the boat will capsize if it hits a strong current."

"Robert Dunn wants us to investigate the origins of that captain. He suspects the man might be a Bolshevik spy using his position as a cover," John interjected, pushing his hat off his forehead.

"A cover for what?" said Connie, easing herself upright. "Why would the Bolsheviks care about what goes on in Istanbul?"

"The city has become a hub of political activism. Concealed among those refugees are numerous White Russian sympathizers loyal to the late czar."

"How does Dunn know these things?"

"He's an intelligence officer—that's what he is supposed to do, my dear." There was a hint of condescension in his voice; Connie glared at him.

"Have I met this Robert Dunn?" I asked.

"I doubt it. Bristol only just brought him on board, if you'll pardon the pun," said John; he smiled at his wife as if to reassure her of his love. "You've missed all the excitement, Mary. Bristol finally received his longed-for promotion to high commissioner. He immediately brought in Dunn to head intelligence."

"You'll be pleased to know Dunn is very sympathetic to the Turks," said Connie.

"...and a Muslim convert from Buddhism," said John, with a hint of a smile. "A canny guy, not stupid, but he has some strange ideas. We professional diplomats cannot figure him out."

"Where did he come from?" I murmured.

"At one time he was a journalist in India. I have no idea where Bristol met him. I don't have a lot to do with that department."

"Would you mind asking the cook to make fresh lemonade? The gardener picked a batch of fresh lemons this morning," Connie said to John, giving a languid wave toward the house. "I am too lazy to get up."

"Are you hot? Perhaps we should go inside," said John, placing the back of his hand against Connie's forehead.

"Lemonade will cool me down," she said with a sigh, part exasperation, part contentment. Leaning back against her chair, she closed her eyes.

"Don't stay out here too long."

John rose, removed his hat, and walked into the house through the French windows.

As soon as he had gone, Connie stirred from her feigned sleep and leaned toward me in a conspiratorial way.

"I think I'm pregnant," she whispered.

"That's wonderful news."

"Sssh, don't say anything—it's my secret. I haven't told John yet."

"Why not? Aren't you happy about it?"

"If the test is positive I'll be ecstatic. I'm not telling anyone else until I am certain."

"When will you know if…?"

"Tomorrow afternoon the consulate doctor is coming here to examine me. If the results are positive, I will tell John."

One look at her face told me all was not well.

"If I am pregnant, I have already decided I cannot have the child here in Istanbul. The city is riddled with disease. Every day the consulate receives new reports of outbreaks of cholera, typhoid, and God knows what else."

"There's a flu epidemic in New York," I said. "It's all over Europe."

"I'll take my chances. The child must be born in America." She lowered her voice so I could barely hear her over the lapping of the Bosphorus against the wooden quay. "Don't misunderstand me. If I am carrying a child, it will be the answer to my prayers. I miscarried in London. Don't look so alarmed; it was early. John was devastated."

"He will support you whatever the outcome," I said. "He adores you."

Her fingers twisted in her lap, and she turned her face toward the house and sighed.

"This posting means so much to him. You should see the look on his face when he's reading the dispatches from Washington or discussing the latest news from Paris with his colleagues."

"If John can't go, I will return to America with you."

No sooner were the words out of my mouth than I was struck with a lightning jolt of clarity; I did not mean what I said. Conflicted, I stared at the ground.

"If John cannot come he will find a companion—his assistant or one of the secretaries' wives."

"But I am your sister."

"And you feel it's your duty? No, Mary, stay. New York holds only sad memories. Bringing you here was best thing I could have done."

Taking her in my arms, I laid my head against her shoulder and heard her heart beat. I blinked away tears as we embraced.

The following day the doctor confirmed Connie was three months pregnant, just as she had predicted. John was overcome with happiness. We toasted the news with champagne hastily dispatched from the French summer consulate, but my joy was tempered with a sense of emptiness that caught me by surprise. Burnham and I had discussed having children in the same detached manner we talked of moving to a larger studio or taking a holiday in Maine instead of Provincetown. In those days our work was our primary concern; color, form, texture, and expression excited us more than the prospect of children. We were careful with our lovemaking, but mistakes happened. I knew too many couples flung unwillingly into parenthood by accident of passion. Naively I was convinced that fear protected me. Then it was too late; Burnham's death put an end to any thought of motherhood.

# 15

When September came around, the peace negotiations resumed. Debate over the Turkish Treaty immediately ground to a halt, but Admiral Bristol was like a terrier that would not let go of a bone. Turkey must remain unified, he insisted. If Anatolia were divided, the stability of the region would shatter. Yet Washington continued to ignore his insistent dispatches.

Hundreds of miles east of Istanbul another Nationalist conference convened in Sivas, deep in the interior of Anatolia. Goaded by the British, the Ottoman government dispatched Kurdish tribesmen to disrupt the meeting and arrest Mustafa Kemal. At the last minute the plot was discovered by the Nationalists, and the embarrassing spectacle of the government appearing to support Kurdish independence led to its immediate collapse. Sensing his support among the people was waning, the sultan called for new elections and appointed a Nationalist sympathizer to be grand vizier. Ottoman Greeks renounced their allegiance to the sultan, and the chasm between Christians and Muslims grew wider yet.

During these tumultuous times, the atmosphere in Halide's house was buoyant; the Nationalist cause was gaining momentum. The sultan and his advisers became increasingly desperate as thousands flocked to support the Nationalist army. The Allies were tense, conscious that the forces assembling were beyond their control. In mid-September the staff of the American Consulate left the summer quarters to address again the future of the Ottomans.

Our habit of going to the soup kitchen in Eyoub every Thursday continued no matter how tense the political situation. One mid-September day, the skies were clear and the shadows on the courtyard black against the glistening stone. A stranger appeared at the gate, his face half concealed by a scarf. Beneath the plane tree the stranger stopped and plucked one of the gold-brown leaves, holding it in his palm as if it were a treasure. His scarf slipped, revealing a familiar profile.

"Can it be?" said Halide, dropping her ladle.

After endless weeks of waiting, there was Mustafa. His face was thinner and burned by the wind, and the lines around his eyes had grown deeper.

"You must tell me everything, but not here," Halide said, taking in the last of the refugees waiting in front of the table.

Stunned, I could not speak, but my face must have betrayed my feelings, for Mustafa put his hand on my arm; his fingertips skimmed my exposed skin. The gesture was quick, but he had never touched me that way before.

"I didn't know you were still staying with Halide Hanim and helping with our work," he whispered. Behind his eyes I thought I saw other feelings. Confused, I started to scrape the last of the rice from the bottom of the tureen.

A disheveled man shuffled to the table and thrust his plate toward me. He was fair skinned; a dirty woolen hat was pulled tight over his head and his unruly beard waved almost to his throat. I took him for a

Circassian or one of the White Russians. Shoulders hunched, he slouched away. Just as he reached th shade of a large plane tree he looked back at me with such utter hatred I felt as if my skin was covered with a thousand crawling insects.

The man squatted at the base of the trunk and began shoveling food into his mouth as if he had not eaten for a week. Although thinner and more disheveled than the last time I saw him, there was no mistaking the vagrant's identity. It was the sergeant. With a start I remembered Tompkins. Had the two of them been in touch?

"Don't look around," I whispered to Mustafa. "Sergeant Parks is sitting over there beneath the tree."

"Are you sure?" said Mustafa.

"I'd know him anywhere."

"I sensed there was someone following me."

Parks glanced up; his animal instinct warned him he had been observed. Within seconds he scrambled to his feet and hurried off toward the gate. Mustafa lost precious minutes dashing around the table and through the crowd of stragglers still waiting for food. By the time he reached the gate, the sergeant was at the far end of the lane, where he hesitated before leaping over the wall into the rambling graveyard of Eyoub.

By now two more men from the soup kitchen had joined the chase. I ran after them, heedless of my own safety. They vaulted over the wall and disappeared into the tangled undergrowth. Silently I cursed the limitations of my sex; my skirt and shoes were not made for running. I found myself in a shaded lane beside fallen tombstones tangled with brambles; here and there I glimpsed a gleaming pillar of stone marking the recently dead. Cypresses gave way to evergreens, and the air was filled with the scent of pine. The path dwindled, and I was confronted with a terraced hillside and lines of gravestones surmounted with swirling turbans. An unnerving silence tightened around me. Conscious of being alone with the dead, I turned and retraced my steps down the hill. Seen from this angle the path looked different—the space beneath the trees darker. Underfoot the loose stones made walking treacherous. I was so intent on my descent I did not notice the figure crouched beside a grave.

"The dead won't hear you," he said with calm authority.

"Don't come near me." I thrust my hand toward him to fend him off, but my arm was shaking.

"They're vermin, these people, and you're a traitor." He waved at the shadowy undergrowth enfolding the gravestones tumbling one against another.

"Save your hatred for the politicians who sent your brother to war."

"He never had a chance."

"My husband was killed in France. He'll never live out his life either, but I can't hold it against every German who walks the face of the earth."

"He's with me; I hear his voice all the time." He tapped his skull.

"I know," I said, desperate to calm him. "I see my husband in my dreams; he's always with me too."

"Where's our Thomas?" he said. His face twitched, and I felt a pang of pity.

"He's lying at peace with all the heroes of that awful war," I persisted.

"They're all around," he said, wrapping his arms around his torso. "In the air, the sky, the trees—they're calling to me, revenge, revenge."

"I've been to the Allied graveyards. They're peaceful..." My voice trailed off as I caught sight of Mustafa at the top of the path. Sensing his presence, the sergeant started and his eyes narrowed. "Filthy Turk, scum of the earth."

Then everything happened so quickly I didn't have time to react. Sergeant Parks darted down the path. Mustafa followed with the speed of a mountain lion. As Mustafa passed I saw a flash of silver—a knife clutched in his hand. The path plunged into a narrow ravine, and the two men disappeared from view. I heard the crash of breaking wood, and then someone screamed.

It didn't take long to reach the edge of the bank. The ground fell away toward a stream. The sergeant was lying face down in the water, blood streaming from his head. Mustafa was wading toward him.

"What happened?" I said.

"He slipped, hit his head on the stones."

"Is he dead?" I edged closer.

"Look away," said Mustafa, his voice firm. "I'm going to turn him over."

"For God's sake, be careful." I clenched my eyes, fearful the sergeant might rise up and shoot him.

The sergeant was dead. Ironically, the accident prevented Mustafa from killing him before my eyes, and I was grateful to be spared from witnessing another death.

The stream flowed crimson. The body resembled a sack of rags shifting with the flow of water. I felt sorry for Parks, dying far from home—another victim of that hideous war. Closing my eyes, I saw the parchment face of Mustafa's son, his blood drying on the cobbles. So the lunatic universe had turned full circle.

The following day Halide received a call from Zeynep Hanim, a journalist who worked for the opposition paper *Tanine*. The reporter had just finished an interview with General Milne, one of the senior British officers. In the course of their discussion the general revealed that the British were about to issue a warrant for Mustafa Pasha, charging him with the murder of Sergeant Parks.

"It's the excuse the Allies have been looking for," said Halide, who was obviously concerned. "Now they are free to issue warrants for each and every one of us who have been associated with Mustafa."

"I was there," I said. "I saw what happened. I will go down to headquarters and make a sworn statement."

"It will do no good—they will arrest you for complicity," she said. "One way or the other, the Allies are determined to silence us."

A feeling of cold helplessness crept through me. Faced with the brute force of authority I was powerless. Truth was relative; what happened that day was subject to the interpretation of the accused and accusers. I gave Halide a look of muted fury.

# 16

At sunrise on the following morning, Halide and I were on the ferry to Scutari, an old Turkish neighborhood at the mouth of the Bosphorus, on the Asian shore. The ancient Greeks called it Chrysopolis, city of gold; the armies of Alexander the Great had camped here on their long march to the East. A succession of invaders from Asia had pushed westward across the plains until, centuries later, they reached the stony shore. Persian kings and Turkic warriors had looked covetously across the churning waters toward Byzantium, glittering on the peninsula of present-day Istanbul. Now the quiet streets of Scutari echoed with the footfall of Allied soldiers.

Halide and I sat on deck with the watery sun warming our faces. She had insisted that I accompany her on this journey she had made alone many times before. We were headed for a dervish monastery, the first stop on the underground escape route. As the ferry started downstream, the shores of Europe receded. The Bosphorus widened before us and curved toward the Marmara Sea.

"There's Sultantepe; it's that steep hill about a mile up from town," said Halide, pointing toward the shore.

Shading my eyes, I peered at the mauve-green hills rising in waves above the town. Sheep dotted the meadows, and the distant clang of cattle bells cast a dreamlike air over the landscape.

"See the mansion on the other side of the wall? Our family and household moved there after we left Beshiktash. My father still lives there."

Set apart, sequestered by stone walls and an orchard, was a white-gray mansion; from the vantage point of midstream it looked like a gothic doll's house.

"My grandmother loved these old, rambling mansions no one else wanted. She preferred living with the spirits of the past," Halide said.

An Allied warship passed close to our port side, waves from the wake rushing against our hull. The ferry heaved violently, and I was thrown against Halide. She grabbed the handrail to keep her balance and then shook her fist at the churning water.

The warship raced toward the Marmara Sea as our ferry glided in to shore. Gulls screamed overhead. Ragged boys on the quay swarmed around the disembarking passengers. Halide removed her cloak and handed it to a pasty-faced child no more than ten years old. He placed it in a basket strapped to his back and then looked at me with his head pitched to one side, like an inquisitive sparrow.

"Put your scarf over your head," Halide cautioned. "They are not accustomed to foreigners around here."

"Are we walking?" I asked.

"There's a carriage waiting on the shore road."

We ambled through the crowd of dispersing passengers. Here in Scutari there was none of the agitated bustle of the European side. The far end of the square was dominated by a mosque flanked by wooden houses pressed against the outer walls. Close to the marble fountains, where the men washed before prayer, a bustling street market overflowed. A trio of fishermen clustered beneath a tattered umbrella, guarding boxes piled with silver-gray fish. They waved as Halide passed. We mingled with the crowd flowing into the mosque. At the foot of the steps an imam, magnificent in white robes and turban, touched his hand to his heart.

"*Merhaba* Halide Hanim," he said in a deep voice.

"*Merhaba amca*," Halide replied, looking thoughtful.

"Everyone knows you," I said.

"Keep your voice down. That man in the *calpak* is an Allied spy."

I glanced tangentially at a stranger leaning against a streetlamp smoking a cigarette. Halide increased her pace, and the boy skipped along behind her, his basket flopping up and down on his narrow back.

Our carriage was waiting by a break in the sea wall that separated the rocky beach from the road. Hooting with joy, the boy skipped away clutching the odd-shaped coins Halide had given him. I found myself sitting across from a stranger in a green turban and flowing white robe. Sheik Muttalib, master of the Uzbek *tekke*, greeted me. His elongated face and shadowed eyes made me think of El Greco's Christ at Gethsemane. Our formal greeting concluded, Halide and I sat in silence, while our companion swayed back and forth humming to himself.

We bumped along a rutted road; although the curtains were drawn, I knew we were staying close to the water because I could hear waves lapping against the sea wall. After a few minutes the carriage abruptly stopped at the bottom of a steep hill. The sheik lithely jumped out, and we followed him up a cobblestone road into the rough driveway of a wooden house almost drowned in an avalanche of wisteria. Cascades of purple flowers tumbled over the roof and along the walls; the windows were hidden by twisting vines. Framed in the doorway, with his hands on his hips, stood Mustafa.

"Welcome to the monastery of the Uzbeks," he said, giving us a broad smile. As we were about to enter, the dervish whispered to Halide.

"The secret password is 'Jesus has sent me,'" said Halide.

"Jesus?" I was bewildered. "You mean our Jesus of the New Testament?"

"Yours and ours; he is one of our most beloved prophets," said Mustafa, smiling.

How little I understood then where the pieces of my new life and my old life would intersect.

After removing our shoes, we were ushered into a spacious hall devoid of furniture. The walls were paneled with white painted wood and the stone floor was covered with a threadbare carpet. Rings of amber prayer beads were laid out in rows on the recessed windowsills. The day was bright, but the wooden shutters were closed, and light seeped between the slats.

"This is the meeting hall," Mustafa said. "You are probably the first foreign woman to set foot in this sacred precinct."

"I am honored," I said, conscious of his eyes on me.

"By virtue of your actions, you are welcome."

A young woman in a headscarf brought a samovar and tea glasses and set them on the floor in front of us. Following Halide's example, I sat cross-legged on a folded rug and listened while the sheik talked to Mustafa.

"If the escapees are known to the sheik they stay in his living room," Halide whispered. "He is risking his life, but he's telling Mustafa it is his sacred duty to take care of his brother Nationalists."

"What about the sisters?" I joked.

"The Uzbek do not differentiate." She frowned at my levity and put her fingers to her lips.

"Since there are Allied patrols on the main road, I'm going over the route before it gets dark," Mustafa said, rising. He pushed open the door and wind gushed in.

"That's the back lane to Camlica," Halide said. "I used to wander there with my grandmother, God rest her soul."

"There is a magnificent view from the summit," said Mustafa, beckoning to me. "Come let us take a walk up there."

"Go with him," said Halide. "I'll join you when I've finished talking to the sheik."

As I followed Mustafa into the garden, my emotions were in turmoil: what was I getting myself into? He was married; no matter how strong our attraction, the image of his sad wife haunted me. I was alternately angry with myself yet curious. We walked through the vegetable garden. Tidy rows of cabbages, onions, and squash gave way to an apple orchard, there the path dwindled into a grassy track. Mustafa strode ahead, swinging his arms; beyond the orchard we went, and up a steep hill, pausing only beneath a canopy of trees. A breeze blew up, shaking the rust-colored leaves.

"Can you make it as far as the top?" he asked.

I shaded my eyes with my hand and looked at the open hillside.

"Is it safe for you to walk out in the open?"

"People here hate the occupiers. I do not fear betrayal."

The sky was cloudless, blue and clear; all around, the countryside was tinged with the promise of winter. After walking for close to half an hour we stopped. I was out of breath. Above the murmuring rush of wind I heard music, like the plaintive song of Pan.

"The shepherd's flute — the song of the reed," said Mustafa, turning his head, "wherein all the secrets of union and longing are contained."

"You are talking in metaphors again."

"The image comes from the songs of the dervishes."

"Halide told me your father was a Mevlevi."

"A master, and a remarkable man. It was he who insisted that I receive a Western education, over the objections of my grandfather."

He lifted his hand and shaded his eyes against the sun so he might see me more clearly. "I am blessed. I was not compelled to follow family tradition. Do you think that is a good or bad thing, Mary Hanim?"

"In general it's good to break free—follow our own path—but I am talking from the point of view of an American."

"Who has stepped beyond traditional boundaries." He gave me a knowing smile. From the way his gaze rested on me I knew. I knew then the attraction reached beyond friendship.

We reached a wall where the shepherd sat playing. Seeing us, his mouth fell open and the pipe tumbled from his lips. Leaping to the ground, he grabbed the pipe and raced away, weaving through the sheep.

"Did we upset him?" I said, watching him disappear between the folding hills.

"You're an unveiled woman—an infidel—and he has just seen your face."

"I walk in the street every day without covering myself."

"He is probably a peasant from the interior, where life has not changed for centuries. Men like him will fight to the death to save our land from occupation, but the greater struggle will be to teach them the new ways."

With a single stride he mounted the wall and extended his hand. As he drew me up beside him I was struck by the strength of his grip.

On the far shore of the Bosphorus the hills of Europe looked gold in the muffled light of the afternoon sun.

He was standing close beside me now. As our arms brushed against one another I felt that familiar frisson that precedes passion—a feeling I thought long dead and forgotten.

"I have not been blind to the way you look at me, nor deaf to the softness in your voice when you speak," he said, giving me one of those looks that bored into my soul, leaving my heart exposed and vulnerable.

"Am I so transparent?"

"Is love a secret? Life is too short. Why pretend?"

"Then you feel as I do," I said, emboldened by his gentleness. "We women sense these things but...you are married."

"Poor Gul is no longer a wife; now that she has suffered the loss of our son, I fear for her."

"What are you trying to tell me?"

"This celibate life has been harsh."

He held me with such longing that I moved to kiss him, but he turned his head away.

"I love you, Mustafa. I never thought I would feel this way again."

"This feeling your Western poets call love is a kind of madness that grips the soul and fells it like a tree in a storm."

"Halide told me your poets write of love."

"The love they extol is love of God, a selfless, all-encompassing condition of the soul."

"Your poets are all too human," I whispered. His body pressed so close to mine I felt his breath against the skin of my neck. "They understand carnal love."

He leaned over and kissed me, and all the contained emotion I had suppressed for weeks poured itself into that embrace. As we held each other on that windy hillside I felt we had known one another a long, long time. Tears rolled down his cheeks, into my hair. I brushed them away with the tips of my fingers and kissed his eyelids.

"My heart is broken, Mary. My son is dead, and living every day is like sweeping sand from the desert. I don't know how to move forward anymore."

Not knowing how to respond, I held him close and felt his body shudder with grief. Gradually the sobbing subsided. He drew himself tall and looked down at me, his eyes red with anguish.

"Mustafa Kemal has sent for me. I leave before dawn tomorrow under cover of darkness."

"You brought me here to say goodbye?"

At that moment I would have followed him anywhere.

"I could not leave without seeing you one last time."

"So this was planned? Halide knows?"

He nodded.

"She did not say a word."

"Halide Hanim and I have been friends since childhood. I would trust her and Adnan with my life."

"Adnan too?"

"After all we have suffered, you and I, they wish us only happiness."

A bird hovered in the clear sky, its song echoing across the hills where the sheep grazed and the shepherd watched from a distant tuft of grass. Far below, the Bosphorus shone like a silver ribbon, and the hectic water traffic seemed like the buzzing of mosquitoes on a pond.

Halide and I rarely spoke of Mustafa, as if reflecting on their past meant revealing secrets I was not yet meant to share. We lived only in the present, exchanging smiles or a complicit nod when his name came up. The specter of Gul stood between us, and I had no desire to resurrect the past. I stayed on in Rumeli Hisar. Connie and I talked on the phone every day. Since Halide's line was tapped, our conversation was guarded. Much to my relief, my sister was not starved for feminine company. Admiral Bristol's wife, Helen, had arrived the previous week, and Connie was full of news of her new friend.

Meanwhile I was working from morning to night; my painting had taken on a life of its own, alive with the displaced energy of desire. I began a painting of a dervish, an imagined figure, standing beneath a fig tree that stood at the corner of Halide's vegetable garden. This tree was said to be haunted. The servants refused to go near it, and the ripe fruit was left to rot on the ground. My dervish stood mired in the rotting fruit, staring at the horizon, toward Anatolia. He had my face, and his eyes were filled with the tears I could not shed for Mustafa. Images streamed from his head, as if his turban had become unwound and was blowing wild in the wind. They were my dreams, waking and sleeping—the thoughts that invaded my mind during the long days after Mustafa had gone.

In early September John returned alone to the Palazzo Corpi; Connie preferred to linger in the cool clear country air in Tarabya. Time weighed heavy on her hands. There was nothing to do and, although I visited every afternoon when my work was done, she longed for more company. Within a couple of weeks she followed him back to Tunel. I was in a difficult position. Now that Sergeant Parks was dead, the danger had passed, and there was no reason for me to remain at Rumeli Hisar. I longed to stay, but my sister was four months into her pregnancy. Nauseated, she needed me, but selfishly I didn't want to feel obligated to return to her side.

# 17

In fall 1919, a Nationalist sympathizer was appointed grand vizier; parliamentary elections followed, and the new Chamber of Deputies was overwhelmingly in favor of the National Pact, which demanded independence and democracy. Although their goals of independence and democracy were evident, I did not fully comprehend how revolutionary their demands were. For more than five hundred years Islamic law, the sharia, had been interwoven into the legal and political system of the old empire. The sultan was God's representative on earth, and daily life was governed by the call to prayer and the rhythm of the Islamic calendar. Kemal and his colleagues sought nothing less than a complete rout of the old ways.

I was not alone in my ignorance. Although the Ottomans had loomed large in the history and imagination of the West, at the end of the First World War almost nothing had been written about their way of life, their past, or their language, with its mysterious tenses and harmonious balance of sound. All of this was unknown save to a few scholars and diplomats. Those decision-makers who thought it their God-given right to resolve the future of the region had scant knowledge of the complex philosophies of Islam, the mystical practices of Sufism, or the basis of a faith that governed the lives of a million simple peasants.

To this day my eyes brim with tears at the memory of this ignorance and arrogance that led to the deaths of a gifted soul like Burnham, the innocent Halil, and even the tragic Sergeant Parks.

Admiral Bristol had been absent for most of that summer working on the Smyrna inquiry that concluded the violent and unjustified occupation by the Greeks and only served to harden Turkish Nationalist sympathies and destabilize the region. Asked by the peace commissioners in Paris to find solutions, Bristol and his colleagues suggested, among other things, restoring Turkish civil authority and replacing Greek troops with Allied forces. But Lloyd George was infuriated by the criticism of the Greeks, and it was only a matter of time before he made sure the report was suppressed.

Bristol returned to Istanbul, his negative views of the Allies confirmed by the testimony he had heard during his stay in Smyrna. Since we did not officially have diplomatic relations with the Ottomans, America and the consulate were neutral. In private, our diplomats expressed cautious enthusiasm for the Nationalist victory. We all wondered how the British would react to a sudden influx of Nationalist deputies into the capital—a solid phalanx of support for Kemal and his revolutionaries. When parliament reopened in January 1920, tensions in the city rose; the delicate threads of order were stretched thin.

Halide did not participate in the election, since the right to vote was limited to Ottoman men over the age of twenty, landowners, and the educated elite. The vast peasant underclass had no say in the selection of a government. It goes without saying that women did not count, no matter what their rank or status. From a contemporary perspective these limitations appear onerous; at the time the overwhelming vote was a cause for celebration. Dr. Adnan was appointed Minister of Health, and Halide's joy gave way to concern. As a member of the government and a known supporter of nationalism, Adnan became a target, not only for the Allies, but also for fanatical supporters of the sultan. Halide was so concerned about their safety she sold her house on Antigone, an island in the Sea of Marmara, to free up funds in the event she needed to send her child out of the country.

Hundreds of miles to the East, Mustafa Kemal was growing impatient; the success of the Sivas conference convinced him he had to weld the disparate Nationalist groups into a united political force. Kemal, the master organizer, decided to set up his headquarters at Angora, a hill town in Central Anatolia, once the center of the wool trade. Kemal disliked Istanbul—the city was rotten to the core, eaten away by prevailing foreign interests and centuries of Ottoman corruption. To be effective, power must be centralized in the Anatolian hinterland, for true power resided in the hearts of the simple Turks of Anatolia.

Mustafa Pasha was among the loyalists who accompanied Kemal on the arduous journey from Samsun to Angora. They drove in convoy: three open cars battered from wear. When Mustafa later revealed that their gas and spare tires had been supplied by an unnamed American woman rumored to be a teacher in an Armenian school near Sivas, I felt a stab of irrational jealousy. Her contribution was so much more than I could hope to give their struggle.

In Paris the Allied commissioners continued to debate the disposition of Ottoman territories, bickering among themselves and growing ever more mistrustful of each other's motives. No decision could be finalized without the agreement of the United States. Then fate took a strange twist. In late September, while traveling in Colorado, Woodrow Wilson suffered a stroke.

Rumors flew that the president was paralyzed, but no one knew the truth save for Mrs. Wilson, the designated regent, who revealed nothing of her husband's condition. Government business ground to a halt. International diplomacy held its breath. As word of the crisis reached Istanbul, our senior diplomats found themselves excluded from meetings with their Allied colleagues. Wilson's condition had sidelined America, and we were effectively excluded from the peace process.

# Part Two

# 18

It must have been mid-October. The weather had cooled and my studio felt chilly; I was about to return to the apartment to retrieve a shawl when I heard moaning coming from the other side of the door. There was a thud, as if someone had dropped a heavy book. A door slammed, and a woman's voice cried out in alarm. I hurried next door to find John slumped across his desk and Miss Harrison, phone in hand, calling frantically for help. I ran over and was about to feel his forehead when she pulled me away.

"Don't touch him."

A note of panic in her voice stopped me; I saw that she was terrified.

Admiral Bristol had been at a meeting right down the hall. He blustered in, followed by an aide who pulled John upright and put his ear to John's chest.

"Heart's still beating," he said.

"He's on fire," said Bristol, laying his palm against John's forehead. At his touch John's eyes opened.

"My stomach, sir, I'm going to explode," murmured John, wrapping his arms around his abdomen.

"Dammit, where's the doctor?" Bristol grabbed the phone.

"At the French Embassy, sir," said Miss Harrison.

"Bathroom," John said, rising unsteadily. The aide, who was young and strong, helped him into the corridor. I started after them, but the admiral put out his arm to stop me.

"Stay here," he said. "Your sister will need you; it looks like cholera."

*Cholera.* The word hit me like an arctic wind. I sank into a chair, my hands shaking, terrified for my sister and her unborn child.

"To be safe, the building must be sealed until this matter has been resolved." The admiral picked up the phone and barked orders into the receiver. The room seemed to swell with the confidence of his command.

Moments later John returned, his face ashen. Bristol and his aide helped him to the couch and covered him with a shawl. The door flew open. Connie stood on the threshold, and her swollen body seemed to fill the opening. As if in slow motion, she crossed the room. I barred her way; she gave me a puzzled stare.

"What happened?" she said.

"He fainted, the doctor's on his way, but to be safe you must not touch him," I said, slipping my arm around her shoulder.

At the sound of her voice John stirred. "Don't worry, Connie," he said in a whisper. "Take care of yourself and our baby."

A tall, gray-haired man strode into the room. Setting his leather bag on John's desk, he beckoned to Miss Harrison.

"Fetch sugar, salt, and fresh water."

"Dr. Harrold," said Connie, "what are you doing here?'

"I stopped to check on you; one of the guards sent me here straight away."

"John was fine this morning. This happened so fast!" said Connie. The pathos in her voice made me tremble.

The doctor put his hand on John's head and held it there. "Probably cholera."

136

John was muscular. It took three guards to carry him up to the apartment, where they helped the doctor put him to bed. Dr. Harrold showed my sister and me how to apply cool compresses to John's forehead. We soon became adept at feeding him sugared water and salt from a pot shaped like a baby's feeding bottle. Gradually his temperature subsided, and within a week he was sitting up in bed and reading dispatches from his office. Miraculously, neither Connie nor I contracted the disease, but others were not so fortunate.

"I ran into Helen Bristol this morning," Connie told me, leaning across the bed where John was sound asleep. "They put Miss Harrison in isolation."

That fateful morning I had seen a flicker of fear in Miss Harrison's face when the word cholera was spoken aloud, as if she had an intimation of her own fate.

"She idolized John," said Connie, glancing down at her husband's sleeping form.

"I noticed she was unusually devoted," I said.

"John insisted on bringing her from London." Connie lowered her voice. "I saw them once, huddled over her desk. They stood close, their bodies touching. John's hand was on her shoulder."

Her face hardened. I didn't say anything, as it seemed wiser to let her talk.

"I slipped away. They didn't hear me, but I did not forget. It was soon after we arrived here, and John was under a lot of stress. When I became pregnant she asked for a transfer. John persuaded her to stay. Poor thing is paying a high price for her devotion."

City sounds came through the window, drowning the silence that fell between us. When Miss Harrison died four days later, Connie announced she was returning to America to have her child. My new life was coming to an end.

Halide and Adnan moved to their apartment in Tunel. Rumeli Hisar was too remote for the long, cold months of winter. Halide telephoned in early December, and I realized we had not spoken for almost a month. John's illness had driven everything else from my mind.

"Our night visitor returned," said Halide, jolting my memory. That incident in Rumeli Hisar now seemed long, long past.

"Did you catch him?" I said.

"Our new dog scared the intruder away before he had a chance to get into the house. But it must have been a local man," said Halide. "Our back gate is well hidden."

"I am relieved you moved back to the safety of the city—you are so isolated out there."

"We are not safe anywhere, Mary Hanim. Now that Adnan is minister of health we are under constant surveillance."

As if to confirm this, there was a click on the line.

"Come round this afternoon," said Halide, cutting the conversation short.

The sound of her voice brought back memories of Mustafa; the power of my emotions took me by surprise. For the past month the never-ending chatter in my mind had been taken up with the problems of John and Connie. I rarely thought of Mustafa except at night, when I was on the brink of sleep. Now I wondered where he was and if he thought of me at all.

It was early afternoon, and most of the workers in the consulate were at their desks. No one noticed me slipping out through the side door alone and unguarded into in the wide air, where I felt light again. A stranger stood at the door of the gatehouse chatting with the guards. As I passed he disengaged himself and fell into step at my side; I had the impression he had been waiting for me.

"It is Mrs. Di Benedetti, isn't it?" he said. A slight drawl revealed roots from the American South.

"Yes?" I replied.

"Lieutenant Robert Dunn, at your service, ma'am." He touched his forehead and smiled, revealing a line of perfect white teeth.

I shot him a glance. There was something odd about his looks; his nose was dented like a prize fighter's, and his mouth curled upward when he spoke.

"Do you have a moment?" he asked.

"I am going to visit a friend, and I am late."

"Ah, a friend." He gave me a knowing smile. "Admiral Bristol did say you have met some interesting people. I'd like to hear more about them sometime. I have great sympathy for the Nationalist movement."

"The admiral knows more than I do."

"Come now, Mrs. Di Benedetti, you were living in their midst."

"For proud people this occupation is hard." It was hard to be circumspect with his eyes drilling into me.

"They're tough, these Anatolians; I have been in the interior and I know."

"If you will excuse me."

"Please don't let me detain you, Mrs. Di Benedetti," he said, with studied courtesy. "I am confident we will see more of one another."

Giving me a brisk salute, he melted into the crowd.

When I reached the edge of Tunel Square, a trolley car lurched over the crest of the hill and stopped in the open plaza at the very spot where I had disembarked that fateful night. Since that time I had avoided the small square where the shooting had occurred many months before. I crossed in front of the Metro station and turned in to the arcade, now choked with tradesmen and shoppers. The stalls were covered with sparse piles of fruit and vegetables; a man in an apron hacked at a block of white cheese and weighed every morsel on a brass scale.

At the top of the steps I gazed down at the square, shadowed by gray December light. Skeletal trees clustered at the corner, close to the door where I had huddled to escape the eye of Sergeant Parks. The wind blew a loose drainpipe against the side of a house; it hit the wall with a monotonous scraping clack. A woman in black hurried into the square holding tightly to the hand of a small child; they walked over the very spot where Halil had died. As they drew closer I noticed the child had a livid scar across his brow.

Halide's apartment building was in one of those narrow streets behind the Grande rue de Pera. The façade was reminiscent of my hotel in Paris. French windows opened onto small terraces overlooking the street, and wrought iron railings were interspersed with ivy and geraniums. A concierge in a wooden booth surveyed everyone who passed through the main door. As I climbed the circular staircase to Halide's apartment a smell of cooking drifted from an upper floor.

Halide greeted me, explaining she was presently without household help because Nakie Hanim refused to come to Pera and risk daily encounters with foreigners.

"Nakie Hanim is a simple soul," she added, giving me a rueful smile.

In the main living room the furnishings were identical to those at Rumeli Hisar: rich carpets thrown one upon another, divans covered in silk, and low copper-topped tables. An armchair covered in red corduroy was the only sign of foreign influence. Along the walls were a number of sepia-tinted photographs framed in gold and suspended from thin wire.

"Who is this?" I asked, peering at a group of smiling children clad in flounced dresses and ruffled shirts trimmed with ribbons. In their midst a solemn girl in a dark pinafore and long-sleeved blouse sat clutching her hands in her lap.

"I was seven." Halide tapped the glass with her finger.

"How serious you look."

"My mother had died a few months before," she said in a matter-of-fact voice. "To add to my misery, my father made me dress like an English child. How I envied my cousins their bright satins and silks, but father was convinced the power of the British Empire derived from discipline imposed in childhood."

I had never given a thought to the influence of these faraway empires; until a few months before, the notion of empire was alien to me. The longer I remained in Istanbul, the more the weight of the past made its impression; echoes of the shattered empire shaped the lives of my friends and molded the everyday life of the city.

"Such a mass of contradictions," Halide said pointing to a youthful man with the same wide, sensuous mouth as her own. "A forward thinking Ottoman, a member of the elite, and yet he married two women like an uneducated Arab from the provinces."

"Two wives, at the same time..."

"After my mother died his second and third wives were forced to share a house, albeit a large one. The pain and jealousy of that impossible situation has left me with a horror of polygamy."

"Did you ever ask him why he did such a thing?"

"He claimed he did it for me. He married Teyze, my beloved tutor, so she might remain in our household. Under the sharia law of the old empire this practice is permitted."

She turned to me, her eyes unsmiling. "Come, my friend, I didn't ask you here to relive the past. How is your brother-in-law, and how are you?"

She steered me into the living room and we settled onto the divan. Leaning into the pillows, I sank into an ease I had not felt for weeks. Out of nowhere came a longing for Burnham. I saw him, legs crossed, in the paint-spattered trousers and loose shirt he once wore in the studio. Life went on, forever changed, forever haunted.

"Gul Hanim is near death." Halide's voice seemed to echo along an empty corridor. "Latife Hanim called yesterday."

"Poor woman," I said, still thinking of Burnham.

"Death is a partner in our lives," she said as if reading my thoughts. "After her son died Gul gave up. There comes a point when the human spirit cannot fight anymore."

The call of the muezzin drifted through the French doors, thrown open to the afternoon sun. Beset by conflicting emotions, I gazed out at a gull wheeling above the rooftops; in the distance the outline of the old city was blurred by a violet mist. To all outward appearances everything was as it was before, yet all was on the brink of change.

Winter brought an early dusk. As I walked back through the streets tension electrified the air, and the few passersby looked nervous as they hastened homeward before nightfall. Anxiety seemed to stiffen the posture of the English soldier standing at the corner of Tunel Square, and he followed me with his eyes as I hurried by. In the lanes close to the consulate, the sound of my footsteps echoed from the walls as if I were being pursued by my own shadow. In the half-light the gauzy specter of Gul Hanim beckoned to me. The image was so vivid I stopped at the gates of the palazzo panting with fatigue.

Lieutenant Dunn was leaning against a pillar at the top of the steps; as soon as he saw me he bowed, waving his hand in an exaggerated flourish.

"Mrs. Di Benedetti, I've been waiting for you."

"Has something happened to John?" I said, fearing my brother-in-law might have taken a turn for the worse.

"Admiral Bristol would like a word with you."

Robert Dunn touched my elbow as if to guide me up the steps; I recoiled, but he did not relinquish his grasp.

The admiral was waiting in the same reception room Connie and I had retreated to on the night of the shooting. A fire burned in the grate, and he stood warming his hands over the flames.

"Come in, come in," he said, beckoning to us. " Sit down, please."

"It is to do with John isn't it?" I asked, taking the nearest chair and looking askance at Dunn.

"John? No, not John. It is your sister who concerns me," said Admiral Bristol, straightening his shoulders.

"Connie?" I felt my heart tighten again.

"Your sister confided to my wife that she is unhappy in Istanbul and wishes to return to the United States to have her child."

"Can you blame her?"

"In her shoes I would feel the same way," the admiral said, nodding. "John is an important member of my diplomatic team. I value his opinion and want to do everything in my power to facilitate his full recovery."

He hesitated for a moment. "After consulting the doctor I have decided to grant John six months leave so that he can regain his health, and Mrs. Olsen can give birth to their child in the United States."

"That's wonderful news," I said. "Connie must be thrilled."

"I have not yet informed either of them of my decision." Admiral Bristol coughed and covered his mouth with his hand.

"Olsen will be charged with presenting our Smyrna report to the Secretary of State," said Robert Dunn, with the precision of an actor picking up his cue. "It is imperative that this document reach Washington by the New Year. They must depart within the week."

"Won't that depend on John's recovery?" I gasped. The thought of leaving Halide and Mustafa was like a blow to the body.

"The sea air will do him good," said Admiral Bristol.

"I'll help my sister pack, and of course there's John's care," I said, my mind racing. " I don't think I can be ready in a week."

"You must not feel obliged to leave," said Admiral Bristol. "I will make arrangements to see they are well taken care of on their journey."

"I am their guest," I said, choosing my words with care.

"You have made your own imprint here, your own friends—interesting friends—and I am told your painting has benefited from the new environment."

"I would have to discuss this with Connie," I said, wondering how he knew of my work.

"And so it will be when they return in six months. Besides, we have to make time to have our talk."

"What talk might that be?" I replied, wondering what he was referring to.

"You were going to relay to me your observations of the comings and goings in the Adnan and Halide Adivar's household."

"So that's what this is all about." I looked at his steady profile. Not a muscle of his face moved.

"You have gained the affection of Halide Hanim. It would be a pity if that connection were severed. Surely you can paint and observe at the same time."

I paused to consider this. "You want me to spy on my friends."

"Any observations you think will help the United States to maintain a supportive relationship with our friends."

"To be kept in strictest confidence," added Robert Dunn, studying me as if I were a specimen in a petri dish.

"There will be a war, Mrs. Di Benedetti. The Allies ignored our recommendations in the Smyrna report, and the British want to hand the area over to the Greeks," the admiral continued. "The situation is deteriorating. Anything you can tell me about Halide and her colleagues will help me gauge the strength and cohesion of the Nationalists. Our future policy in this part of the world may depend on it."

"My friendship with Halide has nothing to do with politics. I help her feed the refugees at Eyoub Mosque, that's all."

"That's all?" mused Dunn, smiling to himself.

"One of our Turkish informants heard rumors about important documents that were rescued from a courier by an unknown American woman," said Admiral Bristol.

"If that was you, your presence of mind was laudable," said Robert Dunn.

"If that was me," I replied, wondering where I found the nerve to respond with such colossal calm. I bit my lip to stop myself from shaking.

"If it was you," echoed the lieutenant, his manner menacing.

"We've talked enough for one day," said the admiral, tugging on a rope that hung beside the fireplace.

Moments later a servant appeared carrying a tray of drinks and a dish of olives and white cheese. He poured water into silver-gray liquid and stirred the cloudy concoction with a spoon. I scrambled to collect my thoughts. Now that the papers were safely in Anatolia, the only serious consequence of telling him everything would be to my own credibility.

"To life," said Admiral Bristol, clinking his glass against mine.

"To life," I replied taking a sip, the sharp taste of anise soothing my parched throat.

"To peace and justice," added Robert Dunn, who declined to drink.

"Have you told John about these rumors?" I said at length, calmed by the effect of the alcohol.

Admiral Bristol shook his head. "John is a conscientious diplomat and a fond husband. I have no wish to disturb the equilibrium of his family."

"If I were to stay, how would I explain my decision to Connie?" I asked, determined to admit nothing until I had spoken to Halide.

"My wife gets lonely when I am away; she will miss your sister. If you stay, your company will mean a great deal to her."

"I understand," I said, smiling at the image of the self-possessed Helen Bristol pining for her husband.

"Fortunately the Allies know nothing. If they suspected an American woman had assisted the Nationalists, I would be in a difficult position. I am charged with protecting all Americans in this region. Do we understand one another, Mrs. Di Benedetti?"

"I am afraid we do, sir," I said.

An aide entered carrying a sheaf of papers, and their talk turned to speculation about President Wilson's condition. Their voices became a blurred background to my thoughts. If I told the admiral about the papers, being truthful would only confirm their suspicions. If, as it appeared, Bristol and Dunn were sympathetic to the Nationalists, no harm would come of my telling them what little I knew.

That night I waited for Connie in their tiny drawing room. A wintry fog enveloped the city, and straggling clouds hid the stars. On nights such as this the rational thoughts of day gave way to nagging uncertainty. I was working in a vacuum. Far from the influence of contemporary artists, my painting had taken on aspects I did not understand. Why had I become the subject of my own work? Now I was revealing my dreams and thoughts as if I were in a dialogue with myself. What had become of the realist I had been in New York?

The hall clock struck nine, and I heard footsteps. The front door opened and Connie came in looking flushed.

"There you are, Mary. I've been looking everywhere. John told me you were with the admiral. Did he tell you our news?" she said, tossing her cloak on a chair.

"I am thrilled for you," I said rising to hug her.

"So exciting to be going home to America after all these years. I can't wait." She twirled in place, then fell into an armchair, letting her arms flop over the sides like an abandoned marionette. "We're going first class, with an attaché to take care of John. Our child will be born in America; it's the answer to my prayers."

"When do you leave?"

"Soon—there is so much to do I hardly know where to start."

"I'll help, don't worry, and anything forgotten I'll take care of once you have left."

"The admiral told me he had asked you to stay," she said, her expression at once thoughtful yet puzzled, "ostensibly to keep Helen company, but that's a lot of nonsense; she is used to being alone."

"If I tell you the real reason you must promise not to reveal it," I said, on the brink of telling her the admiral's proposal.

"You're not ready to return—I understand," she interjected. "What is there for you at home—an empty life without Burnham, an apartment filled with his absence. No, Mary, you've found something here; you must stay for as long as you wish."

"If you wanted me to go with you, I would understand," I said.

"I'll miss you, Mary, but let's face it, our lives have gone in different directions. You're an artist, and I am to be a mother. If this is where you find inspiration or whatever it is that moves you to paint, then you must stay."

So there it was out in the open; inwardly I blessed her for being so forthright. I walked over to the window and drew the curtains against the night.

"Before you know it I will be back; John is scheduled to return next summer."

"That soon?" I said lightly.

"I have a favor to ask of you."

"Anything..."

"Those new paintings..." Connie hesitated. "I want to take one with me."

"You mean the dervishes?" I asked.

She nodded.

"Which one do you want?"

"The dervish of dreams," she smiled.

"Take it, with my love."

"It will go in the drawing room where all our guests can see it," she said. "As soon as our baby's eyes are open he or she will see what a gifted aunt you are."

Ten days later I found myself once more on the platform at Sirkeci station. Connie stood at the window of their compartment chattering excitedly until the guard blew his whistle. John, swathed in blankets, managed a weak wave. I watched as their train disappeared into a cloud of steam and turned away feeling saddened. Partings still alarmed me; implicit in leaving was the promise of no return. I walked away toward the wintry light that fell in parallel lines through the arched windows above the entrance. Cold air hit my face. I wrapped myself in my scarf and hurried into the station yard, where the consulate car was waiting.

The holidays passed quietly; I missed my family. Christmas was a difficult time to be alone, but Helen and Mark Bristol were very kind.

They made certain that I was invited to every reception and celebration in the consulate, conspicuously placing me next to single men in the vain hope I would meet someone of interest. My heart and mind were elsewhere. Mustafa crowded my thoughts, and I wondered what need was driving my imagination. What hunger had he touched—a need to be desired, or a growing loneliness I was loath to admit? During the gray and dreary days of January it was easy to fall prey to depression. I worked long hours in my studio, but painting is a solitary occupation, and my imagination roamed along troubled paths. January gave way to February, when the bitter cold kept me indoors working on my dervish series.

Connie's letters came intermittently. When they were at sea mail was erratic; on land she used diplomatic couriers. After suffering a relapse in Paris, John was ordered to rest, delaying their journey by more than a week. They stayed at the consulate under the care of an American doctor. Eventually they sailed into New York at the end of January and stayed with our parents at the house on Tenth Street where Connie and I had grown up.

At three o'clock in the afternoon I put away my paints. Beyond the window the sky had darkened, and heavy snow clouds hovered over the city. Despite the bitter cold, this was the hour I liked to walk the city streets, wrapped in a scarf and layers of coats to keep out the cold. Jostling city life cleared my head of dervish images and brought me into the hectic present once more. Today would be different. The admiral had asked to see me without giving a specific reason.

He didn't see me enter. He was leaning over a large map spread across the top of his desk, his back toward the door. I coughed discreetly so as not to startle him.

"Ah, Mary, thank you for taking time from your work. I know how much it means to you." He looked up from the map. "Take a look at this. The French are paying dearly for their incursion into Cilicia."

"I take it those stars have some significance," I said, peering over his shoulder at the region bordering Syria.

"Each one marks the site of an attack by the Nationalist army. Soon the entire area will be obliterated by stars."

"Someone told me these attackers are nothing more than local bandits."

"They are too well organized for common thieves," replied Bristol, shaking his head. "The Allies refuse to admit they are facing a formidable, well-organized force. This Mustafa Kemal is a military genius."

He waved me toward a chair; a pot of coffee and cups stood on a side table. "Sit down, make yourself comfortable. I'll put this away and we can talk."

"Doesn't appear to deter the Allies from pushing forward with their plans to divide the country. Have you heard anything from Paris?" I said crossing the room to a chair.

"My Allied colleagues don't tell me a thing. When the Senate voted against the Versailles Treaty we were out of the picture," he said, leaning back against his desk, clasping the edge with his fingers to steady himself. Gray light streamed through the window, bringing out the crevices of his face; he looked drawn and tired.

"What does Washington think?"

"Our government is at a standstill. The president is incapacitated; no one has seen him for weeks except his wife. The only hope for peace in this region is to maintain the territorial integrity of the empire and help them get back on their feet. It would take a foreign mandate to keep the region together. I send daily dispatches urging the State Department to oppose partition, but no one listens, no one listens."

"The Allies would never agree," I said.

"Allied opinion is not my concern. When he was in good health our president went to Paris and pledged to work for self-determination and a lasting peace. It is my duty to stand by that promise."

"But, Mark," I said, moved by his passion, "who would administer the mandate?"

"America," he said quietly." Politically and economically, we Americans have no claim on this region. I don't trust the Allies."

Taking a chair beside me, he put his head in his hands and sighed. For want of something to do I sipped my coffee and waited for him to speak.

"Heathcote Smythe telephoned me at home last night; for him this was most irregular behavior," he said, sitting upright and straightening his shoulders as if shaking off the weight of the State Department. "The subject of our conversation was you."

"So that is why you asked to see me?"

"Allied HQ suspect you got hold of those papers the boy was carrying before he was shot. Damned decent of him to warn me; this information is confidential."

I took a deep breath and said nothing. Sooner or later I had suspected the Allies might come to this conclusion.

"I have long suspected you were hiding something, but at that time I didn't know you well enough to push you. I assume you gave the papers to Halide Hanim, who passed them on to her colleagues. That would explain your friendship with Mustafa Pasha and his mother."

"Seconds before he died, I looked the boy in the eye, Mark. From that moment on I had a moral obligation to protect those papers."

"Why didn't you tell me at the time?"

"I didn't know if I could trust you. We had never met before, and you represented the authorities. For all I knew, you might have handed them over to the Allies."

"Parks was insane; your life was in danger." He got up and began pacing across the room as if to avoid looking at me; I couldn't tell if he was angry or disappointed.

"I didn't understand how fraught the situation was in the city."

"All the more reason you should not have been wandering around after dark dressed as a Turk."

"What's done is done, and besides, the Allies have no proof; it's all conjecture on their part."

"Heathcote Smythe hinted they have new information, from where I don't know—an eyewitness, an informer, or some poor devil spilling information under duress. The point is, the Allies will now be watching you more closely. Be careful, Mary. My powers of intervention are limited."

"Mark, I am sorry. I don't want to add to your problems; I did what I thought was right, and now I must be responsible for my actions."

"Stay away from Halide Hanim and her friends. The Allies are nervous about the growing power of the Nationalists. They have her and Dr. Adnan under constant surveillance."

"But Halide comes to see you all the time."

"We always meet here, in the consulate. This is American territory outside the jurisdiction of the damned Allies."

"Then I take it I may see her here as well."

"Of course." Mark Bristol relaxed and gave me a gentle smile. "Halide Hanim is a courageous woman. My wife and I have grown fond of her, as we have of you, Mary. We all need the comfort of friendship."

Mark's warning disturbed me; I concluded the informant, if there was one, must have been a colleague of Halide and Mustafa. Not a single soul had witnessed my chance meeting with Halil, of that I was certain. Maybe the Allies were bluffing, pretending to know more than they did and hoping to push me into a blundering confession. To be safe, I stayed close to Palazzo Corpi, taking care to wear a heavy muffler and hat so my features were half concealed when I went walking in Beyoglu. There were more Allied soldiers on the street. They patrolled in groups of two or three, their rifles held close to their sides, their eyes shifting nervously beneath the rims of their caps. More significant was the disappearance of the triumphant blue-and-white Greek flags from churches and storefronts. Even in the European area it was obvious the mood of the city had shifted.

About three weeks after my conversation with Bristol, Halide surprised me by walking into my studio unannounced at nine o'clock in the morning.

"What brings you here so early?" I asked, laying down my brush and wiping my paint-stained hands on an oil rag.

"I have an urgent meeting with Mark Bristol, but I wanted to see you first."

"What's happened?"

"Great news," she said, her cheeks flushed pink, giving her a look of childish joy. "The Chamber has officially adopted the National Pact as policy. There will be a public announcement this evening."

"But what does this mean?" I said.

"This government has made Turkish independence and territorial integrity the cornerstone of its policy. It is an open declaration of defiance."

"My God." I felt the air go out of me, as if I'd been punched in the stomach.

"You were part of this, my friend. Without those papers the process would have been set back for months."

"What will this mean for you and Adnan? He's a deputy—are you in danger?"

"I've lived with the threat of danger for months," said Halide. Her eyes strayed to the bright dervish paintings propped against the wall. "You have been working hard, Mary. These paintings are remarkable. You have captured the spirit of the dervishes."

"You think so?" I asked, my heart still racing from her news.

"Compared with your first paintings, the transformation is extraordinary." She paused before a painting of a woman dressed in the robes of an itinerant dervish. From her head flared clouds of bright color containing portraits of dancers, children, and imaginary gods.

"I once thought of myself as a realist, but now I paint the content of my dreams."

"My beloved grandmother told me our dreams were the truth. The tangible world is mere illusion—a ruined house of fools." Her dark eyes brimmed with tears; she wiped them away with the tips of her fingers. "Forgive me, I am on edge. These memories of the lost past are taxing."

"Will you have to leave?"

"Adnan and I are being watched; we will return to Rumeli Hisar this evening under cover of darkness. I must gather my papers together for the journey home."

"Talking of papers...did Mark Bristol tell you the Allies know I took the papers from Halil and gave them to you?"

To my amazement she threw back her head and laughed.

"What took them so long to put two and two together?"

"The admiral was upset I didn't tell him at the time," I said.

"He was relieved," said Halide. "If you had told him he would have been duty bound to turn the papers over to the British. Believe me, Mary, Mark Bristol admires your quick thinking."

After Halide had gone I sat for a long time staring absently at the hills above Eyoub. Our conversation forced me to confront the fact that I had developed a deep sympathy for the Turkish people, defeated, occupied, yet steadfastly refusing to surrender their land to Europeans.

Burnham's death hardened my feelings. I could never forgive the theft of his life—his genius—caused by this same greed that threatened to divide Anatolia as part of the spoils of war. I didn't think of myself as a traitor, but I was soon to discover that the Allies thought differently.

The room grew cold as another day drew to a close. I packed away my paints and brushes and made my way downstairs to have dinner with the admiral and his wife.

# 19

The following Sunday I started out early for the Franciscan Church of St. Anthony, about ten minutes' walk from the consulate, just off the Grande Rue de Pera. As I was passing the Swedish Consulate I heard a loud noise, like the crack of a gunshot. I glanced up just in time to see a massive branch split from one of the plane trees in the garden and crash to the sidewalk in front of me. It all happened so quickly I did not have time to feel afraid. It was only when the sentry stationed at the gate came running over and began to escort me away that I realized how close I had come to being injured. The fallen limb was the size of a sapling; its shattered twigs lay scattered across the sidewalk. The gash on the trunk was long and raw, like an open wound; at its core the tree was hollow.

I was leaning against the wall shaken by my narrow escape when the quiet Sunday atmosphere was disturbed once more, this time by the sound of marching feet. A battalion of British soldiers rounded the corner, their rifles on their shoulders, their eyes fixed on the road ahead. I had never seen anything like it before, certainly not on a Sunday, when even the Allies relinquished their tight grip and permitted their troops to rest. As quickly as they had come, the soldiers disappeared in the direction of Tunel Square, and I was left staring after them in surprise.

A Turk in a military greatcoat and calpak was standing nearby. Suddenly the wind blew up, sending twigs and dead wood in swirling circles; the Turk licked his finger and held it in the air.

"A nor'easter, unusual for this time of year," he whispered, drawing close to my side. It was Lieutenant Dunn.

"Why are you dressed like that?" I said, irritated by his deception.

"The spirits are restless today," he said, gazing up at the scudding clouds, "disturbed perhaps by the Allied activity."

"What on earth do you mean?" I asked, taking a step back.

"Wind and spirit have the same root in Turkish," he went on. "We Westerners ignore the signs at our peril."

"I didn't know you spoke Turkish."

"Enough to get by."

"Then I'd best leave you to your studies," I said, wondering how to get away from him. Something about him gave me the creeps, but he was a clever man, that was obvious — not a person to cross.

"That is an elegant outfit, Mrs. Di Benedetti," he said, looking me up and down. "Are you on your way to an assignation or simply out for a morning stroll?"

"I'm going to mass at St. Anthony's," I replied in as cool a manner as I could muster.

"Do you mind if I join you? I'm going that way."

I did not respond, but Robert Dunn was not a man who was easily deterred. We walked together in silence. He clutched his hands behind his back, bent his head forward, and whistled under his breath.

"Did you see those soldiers?" he asked.

"How could I miss them? They took up the whole street."

"Peculiar, don't you think? Why are the British moving large numbers of troops through the European quarter on a Sunday?"

"I have no idea," I said, conscious of the curious glances we were receiving.

"Yesterday the quay at Galata was mobbed with Tommies up from the Dardanelles and more gunboats in the Horn," he said, still staring at the ground.

"Gunboats?" I exclaimed, unable to conceal my alarm.

"If I were you I'd return to the palazzo as soon as the service is finished."

"Thank you for your concern, Lieutenant."

He touched his forehead, and I felt his eyes boring into my back as I walked away.

The doors of the church were wide open; I found a place at the back of the nave, but as soon as I sat down the clouds of incense caught in my throat. I stifled a cough. At the far end of the church, suspended above the altar, the figure of Christ hung from the Cross, his bloodied head bent beneath his crown of thorns. Suddenly a sense of impending danger held me in my seat. The voices of the choir swelled, and the congregation rose to greet the procession of priests as they started down the aisle, but I could not move. Fear pressed on my shoulders, pinning me in place; I heard the stamp of marching feet and saw the soldiers' cold blue eyes fixed on the road ahead.

I forced myself to stand and then hurried out of the church, through the courtyard into the bright daylight, driven by the certainty I had to warn my friends. The bell stopped tolling, and the low clamor of the Sunday city murmured above the rooftops. I turned into a side street, hailed a passing carriage, and in halting Turkish directed the driver to take me to the ferry station at Orta Koy.

It was late afternoon by the time I reached Rumeli Hisar. The wind had subsided and the village was submerged in mist. As I climbed the hill toward Halide's house I could not see the road ahead, and the formless shapes of gardens and houses loomed like specters in the fog. I rang the bell and waited, but not a sound emerged from within. I pressed my ear to the door and rang again. The bewildering silence was broken by a steady drip of water falling from the roof. Somewhere in the shrouded garden a bird called. Then through the mist I saw the silhouette of a woman walking slowly up the hill.

"Mary?" said a familiar voice.

"Oh, Halide, I feared I had missed you."

"What are you doing here?" she asked, pushing the door open. As we entered, the scent of rose oil filled my nostrils, reminding me of the previous summer, and Mustafa, and the excitement of unexpected love.

"The British are moving troops into the city," I said, draping my coat over the wooden trunk by the door. "An entire battalion passed me on the Grande Rue on my way to church. I've never seen more than a patrol on the streets before."

"Time for retaliation," she said with a sigh. "Come, let's talk in the comfort of the salon. I'll ask Nakie Hanim to bring tea."

"She's here?" I exclaimed. "No one answered when I rang."

"Nakie Hanim has grown deaf," she said, linking my arm through hers the way I once did with my sister. "The passing of the old world has become too much for her, and she has withdrawn into the safety of silence."

Halide and I talked until we could barely see one another in the gathering darkness; then Nakie Hanim shuffled in carrying a lighted candle and tapers. Oblivious to the two of us, the old lady moved through the room, muttering under her breath. Her hands shook as she removed the glass bowls shielding the gas lamps and lit each wick with a taper. We watched while the flames leaped high, then subsided to a gentle flare.

"We were one of the first homes to get electricity," whispered Halide. "Nakie Hanim disapproves."

"It's as if we had been cast back in time," I said as the light flickered, sending shadows trembling across the walls.

"This half-light takes me back to my childhood," said Halide. "Unable to sleep, I sat by the window in the harem keeping watch for the peris who lived in the well at the far end of our garden."

"You mentioned them before. What on earth is a peri?"

"You call it a spirit, a fairy; they have the power to transform themselves into human form—then they are especially dangerous." Her conviction was absolute, at odds with her intellectual persona.

The front door clicked and footsteps in the hall announced the arrival of Dr. Adnan.

"Adnan thinks talk of the peris is foolish," said Halide, putting her finger to her lips. "He has complete faith in logic and science, the new religion."

"*Iyi aksamlar canim,*" said Adnan, sweeping into the room. I noticed lines of anxiety running down his cheeks; within weeks he had aged.

"What brings you home so early?" asked Halide, addressing her husband in English.

"The coup d'état will take place tonight." His voice trembled, and his usual calm demeanor was replaced by something close to fear.

"Tonight? Are you sure?"

"Word from impeccable sources at British HQ."

"There is not a moment to lose; we must get ready for the next phase," said Halide.

As he sat on the divan he finally acknowledged me. "What are you doing here, dear friend? You must return to the consulate at once; it is far too dangerous for you to be out at this hour."

"Impossible," said Halide, nodding toward the window where the mist and darkness folded together. "Mary must stay with us tonight when we go to my sister Nighar's house."

"I have given my word I will remain here," Adnan responded. "The British will take us in our homes; we will not resist. Otherwise we will go to Parliament tomorrow and let them arrest us there."

"Why not sign your own death sentence while you are at it?" said Halide.

"Let the world witness this injustice," said Adnan.

"The only thing the world will witness is your foolishness."

"It is a matter of principle," said Adnan.

"What principal—surrender and defeat?"

"You must go, my dear, but I am not moving from this house."

"I will not take a step without you at my side."

"I gave my word to Rauf Bey," Adnan insisted.

"We will spend the night at Nighar's and wait to see what develops," Halide pronounced. "I will send for Nakie Hanim's nephew; he can guard the house."

They veered into Turkish, and Halide's tone became heated. The force of her passion filled the room like an electrical charge, and I could tell by his sagging posture that Adnan had succumbed to her will.

When darkness had enveloped the house, the three of us started through the back door and out into the foggy night. Traveling by carriage might have invited suspicion, so we walked through the lanes without a lamp. It seemed like hours before we approached the neighboring village of Kuru Chesme and saw long beams of light moving between the dipping hills closer to the city.

We arrived at the large wooden house exhausted and muddy, our limbs aching. Halide, Adnan, and I collapsed onto the divans set on either side of a copper stove glowing with heated coals.

How on earth would I explain my situation to Admiral Bristol? My absence would have been noticed by now.

"At least you're safe," he said after I telephoned the consulate and explained to him where I was.

"I had to warn Halide. You understand—I know you do."

He hesitated, and I thought I heard Helen Bristol talking in the background. "This coup d'état is a grave matter, and you have put your life at risk."

"I could not let them round up my friends."

"I must think of a way to get you out of there," said Bristol, his voice barely audible over the crackling line.

"Halide says we are safe here for the time being," I said, not certain if this was true.

"Try to call me in the morning. By then I will have a rescue plan in place."

"Don't worry about me."

"I am responsible for your safety. It is my duty." I heard an edge of weariness in his voice and wondered if this time I had pushed him too far.

I woke with a start, disturbed by a vivid dream: Mustafa and I were traveling on horseback through the narrow streets of a medieval city. We were both dressed in the tattered robes of transient dervishes. I sat up and looked around the strange room. At first I wondered where I was, and then the memory of the previous night came rushing back. I realized I had fallen asleep on one of the divans. I was still wearing my

163

street clothes and my shoes. The coals in the brazier had burned low, and white ash fell on the carpet; on the other divan the shawls were in disarray as if the occupant of the previous night had left in a hurry. Along the wall, the shutters were thrown open and white linen curtains waved in the breeze. Everything looked deceptively normal.

Someone had set a tray of fruit and white cheese on a table. The cheese tasted sour, but the fruit was sweet and melted in my mouth like ice in the sun. I was wondering what to do when Halide came into the room; her hair stood out around her head, and her clothes were rumpled.

"At two o'clock this morning the British took over our city," she said in a flat voice. "They occupied the ministries and the Galata Tower; we have no word on the fate of the guards or news of Adnan's fellow ministers."

"Thank goodness you left Rumeli Hisar," I said, taking in the deepened shadows around her eyes. "I dread to think what might have happened if you had stayed."

"I fear for Nakie Hanim and her nephew, but I dare not call," she said, letting her hands drop to her side. "Nighar sent a gardener up to the house to see what is going on."

"What news of your colleagues?"

"The offices of the Red Crescent were raided at dawn. Our workers were threatened at gunpoint; the British wanted to know where Adnan and I were hiding."

"Oh, Halide, be careful," I said. "Obviously they mean to get you this time."

"So it seems," she said. It was hard to tell what she was feeling, the outer shell of her being was so calm. "Remember Haliss, the refugee from Salonika, the one who worked for Adnan? The soldiers hit him with a bayonet until he bled, but he refused tell them anything, brave child. Poor Adnan was overcome when he heard."

"If they are that determined, surely it won't be long before they find out where you are."

"We have a few days. The British are acting alone, without the help of local agents," she replied. "I told Belkis, my youngest sister, to spread the word we have been arrested; that will stop people talking and turn their attention elsewhere. Phone the consulate while the phones are still working," she said, nodding toward the door. "Saib is expected back at any moment; I want to hear his report of conditions in the city."

The consulate operator told me Mark Bristol had left early for Allied headquarters and transferred me to Robert Dunn.

"There's a warrant out for your arrest," he snapped.

"A warrant," I said, sinking to the floor from the shock.

"Once the British commander, General Milne, learned you were an associate of Halide Hanim, there was nothing we could do; even Heathcote-Smythe was powerless."

"What does it mean?"

"They can arrest you on sight, without contacting us," he said. "My advice is to lie low. If the admiral cannot persuade the British to rescind this warrant, I'll come in person to get you. We will make arrangements for you to return to New York."

The receiver fell from my hand and I sat motionless, staring at the wall. New York seemed remote, a half-remembered landscape of towering buildings and crowded avenues.

"Hello, hello? Are you there?" I heard the impatience in his voice.

"I'm still here," I said, retrieving the phone.

"Listen," he said. "To let us know you're safe, send a note to the consulate telling me the bread has been delivered."

"The bread?" I felt as if I had stumbled into a play where all the actors knew their parts except for me.

"Address the notes to me, not the admiral."

I held up my hand in front of my face to make sure I was not dreaming. As I tightened my muscles a vein in my wrist stood out like a bluff and then disappeared into my arm; my flesh and blood were real.

I wandered back into the main salon. The furnishings, the walls, the ceiling, everything appeared out of focus, as if I was swimming underwater. Standing by the open window I took a deep breath; the cold air swelled my lungs and calmed me..

"So you are one of us now," Halide said upon hearing my news.

"What does it mean?"

"You are the enemy; they can shoot you on sight."

"Dunn said he would come personally and rescue me."

"Dunn can't come here," she said, alarmed. "There are British patrols on all the main roads. Every quay, every mooring, every back lane is being watched. They will follow him."

"What else can I do?" I asked. Events were unfolding so fast I did not have time to think.

"You'll come with us to Angora, of course."

"I can't do that, Halide; what about my family, and the admiral? I can't just disappear."

"There's a warrant for your arrest," said Halide, grasping me by the shoulders. "You are a traitor, Mary. They don't care if you're American—you work with me."

"What is the worst they can do? Deport me?"

"True, if they don't kill you first."

# 20

Two days later Halide, Adnan, and I set off in a closed carriage on the first stretch of our long trip to Angora. We left Nighar's house in the half-light of evening. Since Halide and Adnan were well known in the city, they disguised themselves as an ordinary hoca and his wife. The doctor wore long black robes and a white turban, while Halide donned a dark coat and charshaf she fastened over her forehead, leaving her face exposed as was the custom with women of the lower class. I was allotted the role of their servant, a deaf mute from Anatolia. My disability would solve the language problem. Nighar's cook had given me her loose skirt and jacket. She was a substantial woman, and I had added padding around my waist to mask my thinness. Following Halide's example, I tied a scarf over my hair and left my face uncovered.

We each carried a bag filled with food, extra clothes, and false identity papers, counterfeited by a sympathetic printer in the old city. Saib went ahead to buy our tickets for the ferry and arranged to meet us on the quay at Beshiktash. From there we would go to the tekke in Sultantepe. As we prepared to leave, Belkis and Nighar flung themselves on Halide, weeping and wailing with the fervor of Shi'ite women mourning the death of Ali. Halide remained composed. To submit to tears was tantamount to admitting defeat.

Earlier in the day I had sent a letter to Robert Dunn asking him not to come searching for me until the immediate danger passed. I said nothing of the plans to go to Angora.

There were soldiers and policemen on every corner. As we neared the village I noticed ordinary people had ventured onto the streets, but there were few Turks. Close to the quay a pair of British soldiers halted the carriage and peered into the interior. I sat stock-still, my palms perspiring. They waved us on but we did not relax, for the danger had not yet passed. Warships were moored at the quay, and the ferry station swarmed with sailors and military police. I was careful to walk a few paces behind Halide and Adnan and imitated Halide's undulating gait. I adjusted my expression to one of vacant stupidity, for character comes from behind the eyes, and identity can be betrayed with a glance.

Saib was waiting for us near the water. Our disguise was so convincing he had to look twice before he recognized us. After giving Halide our tickets, he bought a packet of pistachio nuts from a vendor standing nearby and gave them to us to eat on the journey. As they were saying farewell Adnan's eyes clouded, and he strode up the gangway without a backward glance.

The wind stirred the surface of the water, sending white-tipped waves crashing against the hull. It was bitterly cold, but Halide insisted on staying outside where the darkness offered protection. The constant threat of discovery was underscored by the presence of three men in calpaks and heavy coats, standing at the foot of the gangway. Though they tried to blend in with the crowd, something about their posture gave them away, and I guessed they were government agents. I realized how quickly I had adapted to my circumstances, like a desert lizard that changes its skin to blend in with the environment.

The ferry master blew his whistle, engines droned, and the crew members readied themselves by the capstans. Suddenly a woman in Western dress dashed across the quay waving her arms. She picked her way up the gangplank and stepped daintily onto the deck. Beside me I felt Halide stiffen.

"Don't look up," she hissed.

"What's the matter?"

"That young woman is my former assistant, Ayesha Hanim. She lives in Orta Koy. What twist of fate has brought her here on this night of all nights?"

Ayesha Hanim started down the stairs to the women's section; at the door she paused and looked back at us, her pretty face first wistful, then puzzled. The ship's horn bellowed, machinery whirled, and waves slapped the sides as the ferry heaved out into the cold night. Ayesha Hanim continued to stare; then, to my horror, she started back up the stairs.

I kept my eyes down, alert to every movement. To distract myself I picked at my fingernails, deliberately dirtied with ash from the kitchen fire. When the woman was almost upon us she stopped, so close I smelled her perfume. From the corner of my eye I saw her plump feet bursting out of her narrow shoes. Halide was holding the bag of nuts on her lap. She put a handful in her mouth, cracked the shells with her teeth, then spit them on the floor, one by one, something the real-life Halide would never have done. Ayesha Hanim drew in her breath, then turned and hurried down the stairs toward the women's cabin. I sagged with relief, but Halide continued chewing pistachios as if oblivious to what was going on around her.

By the time we reached Scutari it was dark and the wind had risen, stirring the water and causing the ferry to lurch dangerously close to the quay as we docked. There were more British soldiers standing at the foot of the gangplank, watching the passengers straggle off the boat. As we disembarked I caught a glimpse of Ayesha Hanim, but she did not see me and I was grateful for the cover of darkness.

Halide and Adnan walked across the quay toward the coast road, where the carriage was waiting. I trailed behind them, my head bowed.

As we passed the mosque I noticed a poster plastered to the outer wall with the single word "Death" printed in English, in large black letters. Something was written underneath, but the script was too small to see, and I dared not stop to read it.

"What was that?" I whispered once we were safely in the carriage.

"These posters appeared overnight," said Halide. "They threaten death to anyone who gives refuge to a Nationalist."

"Death," I said, suddenly terrified.

"Our supporters are resolute; they will not scare so easily," said Halide.

"Not everyone has your reserves," said Adnan.

I was inclined to agree with him but said nothing. The carriage swayed along the coast road, and at that late hour we did not pass a living soul. Halide and I sat taut as drawn bowstrings, alert to every noise, while the doctor slept, snoring softly. Enclosed in the velvet darkness I lost all sense of time, and it seemed like hours before we reached the lane that led to the monastery.

When we dismounted we found the fog had lifted, and a sliver of moon cast faint shadows across our path. We labored up the steep hill, dragging our bags. Close to the tekke I stopped to catch my breath and stole one last look at the European shore, not knowing when I would set eyes on it again. I was saying farewell to my past, to Burnham, and to the life before the war came and shattered our illusory peace.

There were other escapees sleeping in the main hall of the monastery, Nationalists and parliamentary deputies making their escape to Anatolia. Halide and I were taken to the sheik's drawing room on the second floor, where beds had been laid out for us beside a brazier. A maid brought soup and bread on a wooden tray, and we fell on the food like ravenous cats.

"I will not sleep tonight," said Halide, setting down her bowl and clambering onto the window ledge.

"Nor I," I said, following after her, "although I am bone tired."

After extinguishing the lamp, Halide drew aside the shutters; from our window we saw the back lane where I had walked with Mustafa. Beyond was the outline of the hills of Camlica.

"See those lights?" she asked, tapping the glass. "That's my father's house. How strange to sit here so close yet so far. We did not get a chance to say goodbye."

"Can you send word?"

"I dare not, the British will be watching him."

Through the trees we noticed a thin beam of light sweeping across the sky in semicircles; someone was walking up the lane, his flashlight lighting up the bare limbs with arced lines of gold. Halide gripped my arm and drew back into the shadows.

"I pray we are not betrayed," I whispered.

"Seems to be only one man," she said, straining to see into the lane.

"Who on earth can it be at this hour?" I said, pressing my face to the glass. "It is not a soldier; he's wearing a cloak and hat."

As the light drew closer Halide became tense. The stranger rounded a corner and passed close to the tekke, on the far side of the garden wall. Upon reaching the open arch he paused and looked into the garden as if searching for something or someone. The upper part of his face was concealed by the broad brim of his hat, but I could just make out a long nose and jutting chin. Halide let out a cry like an animal in pain.

"It is not possible," she gasped. "Oh Allah, oh grace of God, why are we humans destined to haunt one another in this life?"

"You know him?"

"It is my first husband, Salih Zeki Bey; I have not laid eyes on him for years."

171

"Your first husband?"

"I heard he had taken a house in Sultantepe, but I never dreamed fate could replay the years with such cruel timing."

I looked back at the arch, but it was empty. The beam of light moved slowly up the lane; we heard the click of a gate and the light disappeared. Halide slumped against the window, her face vacant, but her eyes large as if she had seen a ghost. She had never spoken of him to me. She had a passionate heart. I wondered what hurt he had inflicted to cause such a wall to go up between her and the past.

In the depths of night I heard banging coming from the floor below; I was in a fitful sleep, and the noise came first in a dream. Then Halide was shaking me, urging me to get up, but I was too drowsy to respond. Someone tapped at the door, and a young voice called for Halide Hanim.

"A raid; be quick, we must get out of here," she said.

My boots were squashed beneath the divan; I jammed them on my aching feet. After grabbing a blanket I took Halide's hand, and together we crept toward the door; as we pushed it open the hinges creaked like a thousand nails scouring a metal board. A boy no more than ten or eleven was waiting in the hallway carrying a lamp. We followed him along the passage to a back staircase. From the floor below came the sound of doors slamming, and muffled voices; it was hard to tell if they were English or Turkish. The boy paused, and held up the lantern to light our way.

"Where is he taking us?"

"There's a back door at the foot of the stairs; it leads to the garden," Halide whispered.

The boy hurried ahead of us; in the dark the sound of our footsteps was magnified. I focused on moving silently, amazed at how imminent danger concentrated my mind.

Once outside, the musty smell of damp earth filled my nostrils, and the icy air brushed my cheeks. The boy extinguished the lamp; the only light came from a crescent moon. As my eyes adjusted I saw we were in an orchard; the boy moved nimbly between lines of trees, avoiding low-hanging branches that scratched against our clothes as we passed. At the outer wall, we stopped and leaned against the cool stone. Looking back, I saw lights blazing on the lower floors of the tekke, and silhouettes flitted across the windows like figures in a shadow play.

"We can hide next door, in the garden of Suleiman Pasha," whispered Halide. "He's an old friend of my father."

"Won't that be the first place they look?"

"Suleiman Pasha is a distant cousin of the sultan; they will not dare to enter those grounds," she said. "The boy says there is a hollow oak tree in the far corner; we will spend the night there."

"What has become of Adnan?" I asked.

"I can't think about that now," said Halide, her concern betrayed by a tremble in her voice.

The moon disappeared behind a cloud, and we passed through a gate into an overgrown garden. By the time we reached the oak my legs were cut and my skirt ripped. I spread the blanket on the ground, a layer of moss forming a cushion against the cold earth. Feeling tired, I huddled close to Halide, who began to shiver.

"You're burning up," I said, putting my hand on her forehead.

"It's nothing, I'm fine."

"Take the blanket."

"No, no," she protested, "I have my cloak."

The boy laid out four apples in a line on the ground beside us and then ran away. Courageous child, I thought, watching him disappear back behind the wall.

"I'll keep watch; I am too disturbed to sleep," I murmured.

"Me too," she whispered. "I pray Adnan got away."

"How will we know?"

"Our escape will go ahead as planned. By tomorrow word will have reached me of his fate." She patted my hand. "You must rest. We have a long day ahead."

Sleep was impossible—damp seeped through the blanket, so the cold penetrated to my bones. I pulled the blanket tight around me, but it made no difference. Halide sat with her back against the trunk, her knees drawn up against her chest, staring out into the night.

"Strange," she said suddenly. "So strange to see Salih Zeki again on this night of all nights. He must be staying at my father's house. They are still friends."

"When did you last see him?"

"Years ago; by God's grace our paths have never crossed."

"What about the boys?"

"Rarely," she said, letting out a sigh. "Salih Zeki Bey was not suited to be a father. He is a great mathematician; his life is his work."

We sat in silence staring up at the myriad stars.

"It is a sign," she went on. "It bodes well for the future. That time of my life is finished, God willing."

Rubbing the sleep from my eyes, I sat up. Through the misty light of dawn I saw we were in a tangled garden enclosed by an ivy-covered wall. As I stirred, Halide put her finger to her lips and pointed toward a gate no more than twenty feet from our tree.

"There should be a carriage waiting for us."

"What about the English patrol, supposing they are still in the tekke?"

"If we encounter any soldiers, stay calm. Don't catch their eye—most of them are boys, and they won't have the wit to see through our disguises."

A light mist hovered over the garden, and the chilly air was damp. I pulled the blanket close around me and hurried after Halide, who was already halfway toward the gate. As soon as we were in the lane I recognized where we were. Mustafa and I had been there together just weeks before. The memory revived uncomfortable feelings of desire and longing.

A battered carriage waited in the shadow of the wall, its black painted body sagging so low on its rusty springs I feared our weight would drag it to the ground. The driver sat up front on a slatted seat, his back toward us so his face was hidden. He did not turn around. We were about to get in when we were unpleasantly surprised by a stranger emerging from the darkened interior, rubbing his eyes as if we had disturbed his sleep. It was a gendarme, his uniform disheveled, his boot laces untied. The moment he saw Halide he crushed his cap on his head and snapped into a salute. They exchanged a few words. Halide's eyes brimmed with tears. Fearing bad news, I reached for her hand to comfort her.

"Adnan and the deputies got away," she whispered. "Don't be deceived by these tears, they are from relief. I could not sleep for worrying."

"Where are they?"

"On the mountain road. We will meet them in Yalniz Selvi as arranged." She beckoned to me to get in after her. "There's not a moment to lose. The gendarme will ride to the edge of the village, then we are on our own. He will meet up with us again close to our destination."

"The police are in on this?"

"They are loyal Turks, like us. Our old friend Remzi Pasha is the commander of the Scutari gendarmerie and a devoted nationalist. If we didn't have him on our side, none of the escapees could get through this area alive. The British are watching all the roads out of Scutari."

"And the driver, can he be trusted?"

"He is a prisoner. Remzi Pasha has promised him his freedom if he takes us as far as our first rendezvous."

"Adnan and the others have been escorted over the hills." She assumed a matter-of-fact tone. "I pray they do not run into any patrols." She appeared calm, but I wondered what she was feeling beneath her screen of reserve.

When the carriage slowed, the sun was high in the sky. I rolled down the window and looked out on a windswept crossroads marked by bedraggled trees and a handful of thatched huts. I covered my face with my hand to protect it from flying dust. It was a bleak and lonely place. An English soldier stood beside the road and held up his hand. Behind him three others sat on a bench flashing signals with a heliograph. As the driver reined the horses to a halt, I steeled myself against showing any fear. I leaned on the window ledge and stared into the distance. Beside me Halide chewed on a piece of tobacco and watched as the soldier approached the carriage.

His skin had a yellow tinge and the whites of his eyes were bloodshot. I lowered my gaze and stared at the road. The soldier's boots were worn and dirty, and there were holes in his trousers. Careful British discipline had collapsed out on the unforgiving plain. He took his time looking us over, and I wound my fingers together to stop myself from trembling. Finally he waved us on our way and turned to stare down the road seeking the next group of travelers.

"Excellent," said Halide once we were far enough away not to be heard. "You fooled him."

"Did you see the color of his skin?"

"Malaria."

"Poor thing."

"He was barely older than my nephews," said Halide shaking her head. "I can't help feeling sorry for him; he looked pathetic."

"Lloyd George and Clemenceau ought to come here and see for themselves what misery they have condemned their armies to endure," I said, remembering the luxury of my Parisian hotel.

"They don't care," said Halide. "The war in France was hell, and they sat by while millions died in conditions worse than this."

"In their own backyard," I murmured, thinking of the Allied graveyards sprawled over the hills of the Marne.

The road to Yalniz Selvi passed across a wide plain dotted with clumps of trees and rocks; on the horizon purple mountains rose like jagged teeth. The desolate beauty of Anatolia took my mind off the danger. If character was bound to geography, what hope had armies bred on the green and agreeable pastures of Europe against soldiers raised in harsh terrain such as this? We passed a flock of ragged sheep grazing on the dirt. Close by a shepherd leaned against his stick, and I thought of the hills around Bethlehem. I had never been there, but I imagined the landscape looked much like this.

As the day wore on Halide started to worry about the gendarme, of whom there was still no sign. Without a police escort it would be difficult for two women traveling alone to enter the village. Suddenly the sky darkened and a storm swept out of the mountains, rain hammering against the sides of the carriage. Halide ordered the driver to stop at the side of the road. Despite the sheeting rain, other travelers—donkey carts, soldiers, and peasants—continued moving along the road. Finally the gendarme came running up, soaking wet and agitated.

Shouting to make himself heard above the sound of roaring wind and hail, he explained the delay. Allied troops were on the move; the wires were crackling with information about the latest disbursement. Yalniz Selvi had been taken over by the British that very morning. As Halide listened, her face did not betray any emotion.

"We must locate Adnan," she said to me in English.

"How do we know he's even there?"

"We were supposed to meet in a coffee house," she said, turning to the gendarme.

By the time we reached the edge of the village, night had closed in and the rain had ended. We passed the lone cypress that gave the village its name and rolled into an open plaza bordered by villas and a small mosque. Every building was dark save for the storefront next to the mosque, where a lamp burned in the window. Drawing his pistol, the gendarme dismounted, pushed open the door with the toe of his boot, and went in. The continuous threat of discovery had made me so tense I did not notice how tired I was. When the roll of the carriage ceased, fatigue washed through me, and I slumped back against the seat and closed my eyes. When I came to we were moving again.

"Where are we?" I asked, wiping steam from the window with my hand.

"The villagers got word the British were looking for us. Fearing a raid, they fled to the mountains. Two old men remained behind; they advised the gendarme to try the house of Nazmi Zia, the painter," said Halide. "His cousin is parliamentary deputy for Ismidt."

Our carriage turned, the horses slowed, and I heard the sucking sound of churning mud. When I next rubbed my hand across the window we were in a courtyard enclosed by low buildings. A voice called into the dark.

"Kim var mi?" (Who's there?)

"Can it be?" said Halide, grasping my arm.

Two men walked across the yard holding a lantern on a pole; in the swinging yellow light I recognized the distinctive profile of Dr. Adnan.

Six of us were settled around the hearth in Nazmi Zia's home; along with Halide, Adnan, and me there were two deputies, Jami Bey and Fuad Bey, and our host, a jovial-looking man with a full beard who reminded me of Santa Claus. A fire burned in the grate, and we sat on sheepskins arranged around the hearth.

"How did you get away from the tekke?" said Halide.

"Fortunately we were awake when the police came," Adnan explained. "Sheik Mutalib kept them talking at the front door while we slipped out the back. One of the dervish apprentices took us to Camlica."

Two women entered carrying a tureen of steaming soup and baskets of black bread; the hard crust tasted like nectar.

"When dawn came we broke into two groups; the others took an alternate route, but Jami, Fuad, and I decided to keep to the original plan," said Adnan, speaking English for my benefit.

"God is protecting us," said Halide.

"Don't count on it," said Adnan. "Three escapees were shot on the road to Samandra yesterday, and more than a dozen villagers have been hung for guerilla attacks on the enemy."

I tightened my grip around my bowl to stop myself from shaking. Now we were beyond the boundaries of Istanbul. We had entered a no man's land where the only protection was our wits.

"What happened to your robe?" asked Halide. The doctor was wearing a pair of plus fours and a loose leather jerkin.

"It was ripped to shreds in the mountains, and Nazmi Bey has loaned me these clothes," he said, nodding at our host.

"You look very fine," said Halide.

"More suited to my character than those robes," he said.

"Come now, Adnan, your brother is an imam."

He raised his eyebrow but did not respond.

179

Halide and I retired to the harem, while the men remained in the selamlik; we were in Anatolia and that was the custom. I was so tired, the moment I closed my eyes I fell asleep. I dreamed I was galloping over the barren hills of Anatolia guided by black hounds that raced beside me like shadows. I found myself in the arms of a stranger; I felt his breath on my hair and his cheek against mine. His skin was like ice. It was Burnham.

"You are dead," I said.

His arms fell to his sides and he gave me a look of immeasurable sadness.

"You are dead," I repeated.

His knees sagged and he fell against me; I gathered him in my arms with the tenderness of a mother nursing her child.

The following morning two strangers rode into the yard at the back of Nazmi Zia's house. During the night it had snowed, and their horses picked their way through the deep drifts with the delicate grace of dancers. Each man wore a long coat and riding boots; rifles dangled from their saddles. Beneath their calpaks their faces were weather-beaten and unshaved. As they dismounted, Dr. Adnan and Nazmi Zia came out of the house to greet them.

"That must be our military escort," said Halide, watching from an upper window of the harem.

"Who sent them?" I asked.

"Mustafa Kemal."

"They look like they might keel over in their saddles," I said.

"They came from Eskisehir," said Halide, "ten days ride from here."

"Ten days?" I exclaimed, "Is that how long it will take us to get out of the Allied zone?"

"If we're lucky," said Halide. For the first time since leaving Nighar's house she sounded weary.

The reception room in the selamlik was simply furnished with divans and bright kilims; the walls were whitewashed and hung with grainy portraits of elderly men in frock coats. Our companions were seated around a brazier, warming their hands. Adnan introduced Colonel Essad and Lieutenant Bekir. They leaped to attention, lowering their eyes deferentially.

"More refugees are expected this afternoon," said Adnan. "Nazmi Bey has arranged for the delivery of fresh horses and supplies; we'll set off at dusk."

"Who is joining us?" said Halide, alarmed.

"Colonel Kiazim, Major Husrev and his brother, and Niam Jevad; I don't know the others."

"With a large group," said Halide, "how will we go undetected?"

"The colonel is taking us through the mountains."

"They are impassable this time of year," Halide exclaimed.

"There's no other way, my dear," he said. "The British have secured the main highways, and there are vigilantes in every village."

The conversation veered once more into Turkish. Halide spoke forcefully. I noticed the men never interrupted her as they did one another; even the colonel regarded her with an awed expression.

On the far wall three windows looked out on the road and the desolate hills beyond. From where I was sitting I could see the length of the street as far as the crossroads. While the others were absorbed in their discussion I noticed three British soldiers rounding the corner by the cypress. They held their rifles across their chests and moved from house to house, obviously engaged in a systematic search.

I alerted Halide, and as always they were prepared. We followed Nazmi Zia into a windowless room paneled in dark wood; apart from a kilim thrown across the floor there was not a stick of furniture. Concealed beneath the floor covering was a lever that opened a hidden door leading to a subterranean room. I felt as if I was in an adventure story. Perhaps it was this storybook aspect of our escape that stopped me from being overwhelmed by fear.

Halide headed down the steps, and we followed. As the door slammed behind us I felt a moment of panic. The room was dark, infused with the odor of damp earth. Fractured light filtered in through a grille in the ceiling. As my eyes adjusted to the gloom I saw Colonel Essad draw his pistol and position himself at the top of the steps. Sounds of muffled voices came from the house; we waited tense with anticipation.

The voices grew louder. Two British soldiers were standing on the grille above our heads so close I could see the holes in their boots. I froze, fearing the slightest movement might give us away.

"No one in there."

"Bloody wild goose chase."

"What we looking for, anyway?"

"Anything suspicious."

"Every bloody peasant looks suspicious."

"Search each house, that's HQ's orders."

"Damn HQ, they're not out here in this bloody snow."

They stamped their feet; pellets of ice fell through the grate and melted on the earth floor in front of me.

"I'm sick of this."

"One more house and we're done."

"Then back to the precinct and a bloody fire."

They walked off, complaining about the cold; every fiber in my body relaxed. Then the door at the top of the stairs slid open. Daylight streamed in and Nazmi Zia was there, smiling.

Other refugees straggled in, some on foot, some in ox carts, concealed under sacks of feed. One of the newcomers had the chiseled bone structure of a Greek god; he was the former governor of a province on the Russian border. I have forgotten his name, but his blue eyes and golden looks reminded me of the young men from Williams College and Yale who swarmed into Northampton on those distant weekends of my college years. I had a sudden incongruous longing for the green hills and lush meadows of Massachusetts. The quad at Smith College, the old elms burnished red and brown in the clear light of autumn, the fallen leaves crunching beneath our feet as we walked to class.

# 21

My saddle was made of wood and my stirrups nothing more than knotted ropes fastened tightly around my feet. Compared with the skill of the Turks I was an amateur rider, but my surefooted horse saved me from injury in those treacherous mountains. I lost count of the number of times the road ended abruptly at a precipice or disappeared beneath a pile of fallen rocks. When the paths became so steep they rose in front of us like sheer cliffs, I clung to the horse's neck and wrapped my legs around his bony rib cage. His Turkish name was unpronounceable, so I called him George Washington, for he was an honest, reliable beast.

There were fourteen of us; we rode in single file led by the colonel. We traveled over mountaintops and through wooded valleys and snowdrifts so deep they reached my knees. Late on the eighth day we straggled into the main square of a sprawling town. Close by, the muezzin called evening prayer. The colonel led us through a pair of rusted iron gates. We halted before a large wooden house painted maroon and green. Along the façade lines of windows glowed gold in the wintry sunlight.

My body ached with fatigue. My clothes were filthy, and when I closed my eyes flecks of light danced on my lids. Someone lifted me from my saddle and carried me into the house. I dimly recall being borne through a long hallway and up a great staircase surmounted by a stained-glass window as magnificent as those in Grace Church. We entered a cavernous room where a fire burned in the grate of a vast stone fireplace. My rescuer laid me on a sheepskin close to the hearth; the warmth lapped around me, and my limbs melted like ice. Laying my head on the rug, I remembered nothing more until I woke to find the fire burned low and the room in darkness.

Pain shot through every muscle as I maneuvered myself to a sitting position. A shadow moved at the back of the room. Someone was watching me. I saw the contours of his body outlined against the wall like a Michelangelo figure sculpted from stone. I folded my arms across my chest to protect myself, for everything had the power to alarm me now.

"You have been sleeping for hours."

My heart stood still at the sound of his voice. It was Mustafa.

"I'm dreaming—this cannot be," I said.

"Stay, you are exhausted," he said, moving to my side. In the glow from the dying fire I saw his face; his beard was thicker than I remembered, and his eyes were webbed with lines.

"So many times I've imagined this moment, and now it is here I don't know what to say," I murmured.

We slid into each other's arms as if the time dividing us had been nothing more than the blink of an eye. His embrace felt familiar; I was safe at last.

"When we received word that an American woman was traveling with Halide Hanim, I knew at once who it was," said Mustafa, stroking my hair. "Mustafa Kemal sent me to the border to meet you."

"How did you get through the English lines?"

"Ali Fuad Pasha drove the British out of Eskisehir; it was easy for me to slip through the retreating army."

"And you knew where we were?"

"Colonel Essad keeps in contact with Angora. I have been to this house many times; it belongs to the local governor."

"You came to meet me?" I said, searching his face. There was a distant look in his eye, like a man scanning the pass for a way across the mountains.

"Mustafa Kemal gave orders." He paused to wipe a tear away from my eye.

"I never thought I would feel this way again."

"We are human and still of this world," he whispered, pulling me close.

The contact of his body made me shiver. We looked at one another, recognizing that what had begun between us on that faraway hillside was growing, pushing the limit of our restraint. He moved back, holding me at arm's length.

"The governor expects me in the selamlik," he whispered.

So I went to the women's quarters, my senses aroused, and feelings had I thought buried were resurrected again, like troubled ghosts.

The women of the harem removed my clothes and bathed me in lavender-scented water. They scrubbed my skin until it tingled. My filthy robes were discarded for a crisp nightshirt, and then they placed me between sheets that smelled of mown grass. I felt like a child again. That night sleep was impossible; I tossed and turned while my body burned, whether from fever or desire I could not tell. In the morning I was soaked with perspiration and my head was on fire; the journey had taken its toll.

The following morning an old woman brought me a loose skirt and close-fitting jacket and showed me how to fasten the scarf beneath my chin so my face was visible. She fed me warm milk and pinched my cheeks to produce some color. Transformed once more, I started down the stairs feeling unsteady. Searing pain shot through my back at every step. The main hall swam in front of my eyes; I could just make out a knot of people standing beneath a chandelier of unexpected grandeur. As I reached the bottom step I stumbled. Mustafa disengaged himself from the group and hurried over. He took my arm, and together we walked outside, where a stunning spectacle confronted us.

One hundred horsemen from the Nationalist army had been sent by Mustafa Kemal to escort our group to the train station at Lefke. They crowded into the drive and packed the lane beyond the gate—fierce-looking men more at home on the steppes than in the placid surroundings of the governor's garden. Their horses were restless; they snorted and pawed at the ground, sending coils of steam into the chilly air. George Washington was waiting for me, eyes rolling with uncertainty in the midst of such a wild cavalry. When Mustafa helped me into the saddle, my head reeled and I slumped forward. Cursing the weakness of my body, I pulled myself upright and took hold of the reins.

Mustafa was a skilled horseman unfazed by his fiery-tempered mount, a nervous animal that leaped sideways at the slightest noise. As we rode away, Mustafa took hold of my reins and stayed by my side as we went into the town. News of the Nationalist victory had reached the outlying areas, and crowds jammed the side of the road. From the top of the minaret the muezzin offered prayers in a strident voice. Though the soldiers wore tattered uniforms they rode through the streets in perfect formation, heads high.

Halide, Adnan, and I were assigned seats together with Yunus Nadi Bey, the editor of Yeni Gun, a Nationalist paper closed down by the Allies. I sat by the window, as the pain in my back had spread to my head and neck. My forehead was soaked with perspiration. Lulled by the movement of the train, I fell into a half-sleep made restless by vivid dreams.

Hours passed. I woke with a start, then drifted to sleep once more. Fear mounted in me. What if this was more than fatigue, and I really was sick. I longed for Mustafa's calm and steady presence, but I had not seen him since we left Lefke.

When the train stopped on the outskirts of Eskisehir I tried to get up, but swept with sudden nausea I stumbled against the seat. Halide glanced up.

"I will fetch Adnan at once. He is in the next carriage with Mustafa."

So he was that close, yet had made no effort to see me. An invisible hand clutched my heart and tightened its grip.

"I'll be all right," I said, not convinced this was true.

"I fear the overland journey was too much for you."

"I need air."

Farm workers and their families, too poor to afford the price of a seat, crowded into the corridor. The smell of dirt and human flesh was overwhelming. Putting my hand across my nose, I stumbled through the crush. The pain in my head was so searing I did not see the crate of chickens in the middle of the aisle. My shin scraped against the coarse wood, setting off a flurry of clucking.

An open platform connected our carriage to the next. Feeling unsteady, I limped across, the sound of rushing wind ringing in my ears. I found myself in an empty corridor; I did not see the guard leaning against the open window. Alerted by the sound of the door sliding open, he stepped forward and barred my way with a rifle. *Should I plead with him or call out in English hoping Mustafa or Adnan would hear me?* I wondered, but at that moment Mustafa emerged from his compartment.

"What happened?" he said, looking down at the hem of my coat. Until then I had not noticed the blood seeping through the layers of clothing.

"It's nothing, a graze."

"A cut is a serious matter." As he moved toward me the guard backed away looking baffled.

"I came to find you. I hoped we might sit together until we reached Angora," I said, the ache in my head returning as if stones were pressed against my skull.

"My comrades and I have much to discuss; the Allies have dissolved parliament and..." he moved close and touched my cheek with his hand, "you are on fire."

"Mustafa I..." I do not remember falling, but I must have landed on my elbow, for when I came around, pins and needles shot up and down my arm. Mustafa was kneeling beside me. The young guard helped lift me, and together they carried me down the corridor. My head fell against Mustafa's chest and I heard his heart beating beneath his jacket.

His compartment was filled with the haze of cigarette smoke. Dr. Adnan and four others I had never seen before were seated around an upturned cabin trunk that doubled as a table. When we appeared at the door they stopped talking and leaped to their feet as Mustafa laid me along the seats. Adnan felt my head, and his gravity alarmed me.

"You have a mild case of malaria."

"Can it be cured?"

"I brought quinine from the city; one of us was certain to succumb. With your permission we will take you back to our compartment and begin treatment at once. You appear to be in sound health; you will soon recover."

"Why me?" I said, not wanting to be a burden to my friends.

"Why not?" he said with a shrug. "You are a foreigner, and conditions in Anatolia are harsh and inhospitable, as the Allied troops are discovering."

I lay in our compartment watching the darkened countryside flash by the window. The night was starless, the air dense. I tried to open the window but the catch would not release. Feeling faint, I fell back on my makeshift bed, but sleep would not come. My mind raced. Burnham's face swam before me. I realized with a jolt that the day had passed without my thinking of him.

A sound in the corridor startled me. Who was moving about the train at this hour? I heard the latch click and terrified, I pulled the covers up to my nose. The door slid open and a man entered. I could see the faint outline of his silhouette, black on black, against the wall. If I screamed no one would hear me above the clacking wheels, so I lay still, watching through half-opened eyes. The stranger moved close to my bed and lowered himself to his knees, where he knelt with his hands pressed together as if in prayer. It was Mustafa.

"You scared me," I said, pushing myself on to my elbows.

"I did not mean to wake you, but I have been worried; sometimes the fever of malaria gets worse at night."

"My mind will not rest. The thoughts rushing through my head are out of control," I said, leaning close toward him.

"You are feverish," he said, cupping my face in his hands.

"Adnan says I am contagious."

"I don't care. I need to touch you." He bent toward me and kissed my brow, my nose, my lips. I wound my sweat-soaked arms around his neck; all the pent-up longing of the past weeks made me greedy for his body. Mustafa reached beneath my robe and pressed his hand against my breast. Our heads moved together, and as our mouths found one another time vanished into the vacuum of desire.

He was a confident and tender lover. I surrendered myself to every sensation — sighing, moaning, drawn further and further into the twilight of delirium. Wrapped in each other's arms, we lay close together. Before long Mustafa was snoring quietly, but I still could not sleep. *If only we might stay like this forever,* I thought, *cocooned in our mutual desire.* As we hurtled on toward Angora the train lurched as it switched rails. Mustafa rolled to one side and I was pressed between the wall and his inert body. I did not have the strength to push him away, so I lay still, half suffocated by the pressure of his torso. With a sigh he shifted onto his back and freed me, and I took a gulp of air and felt my heart pounding beneath my ribs.

"We have arrived," said Halide, dashing to the window.

"On time for once," said Adnan, checking his pocket watch.

"So this is Angora?" I said, moving beside Halide. The quinine was starting to work, and my legs no longer buckled beneath me when I moved.

"We have reached the *kabaa* of the Nationalist movement," said Halide.

"What do you mean?" asked Adnan.

"This was our Nationalist *haj*," said Halide, gazing out of the window.

Following her gaze I saw a castle high on a hill, and below, the roofs of a tumbling town; all bathed in the violet light of dawn. So this was Angora, to all outward appearance an ordinary place. I had imagined a walled city crowded with turrets and domes and fluttering banners like those in the backgrounds of renaissance paintings.

Halide left the window and put her hand on my shoulder.

"Thank you for the many risks you have taken on our behalf," she said.

"We Turks never forget loyalty," said Adnan.

Our conversation was cut short by a shrieking whistle. The train slowed as we drew into the station; through the billowing steam I saw a large crowd waiting on the platform. All faces were turned in our direction. My attention was drawn to an elegant figure in a calpak and tailored greatcoat. His brows were straight, deep creases ran between his eyes, and his face was marked by unusual determination.

"Can that be Mustafa Kemal?" asked Halide, pushing stray hairs off her face. "I hardly recognize him without his military uniform."

"We have not set eyes on him since that day we met on the road to the Sublime Porte," said Adnan.

"Almost a year ago," said Halide, pulling her scarf around her head.

"He left for the interior the day after the invasion of Smyrna."

"Only last spring — it seems longer," said Halide pushing her hair under her scarf.

The outer door of the carriage banged open and we heard footsteps in the corridor.

"Quick, put this over your hair," said Halide, handing me her shawl. Adnan caught hold of her wrist and frowned; her hand went limp and the scarf fell to the floor.

Just then the door slid open and Mustafa Kemal stood on the threshold, stiff and straight, as if on parade. In a single glance his startling blue eyes seemed to take in all that was going on around him. When he reached for Adnan's hand, the movement was swift and decisive. I was struck by his slender fingers and flawless skin, neither wrinkled nor darkened despite the harsh life he must have endured.

When I was formally introduced my hand was shaking, and perspiration trickled down my brow. Mustafa Kemal appeared not to notice. With Halide translating, he thanked me for rescuing their valuable documents — an act of courage, he said. The events of that night had become blurred, and courage was nothing more than instinct prevailing over reason.

# 22

We were driven to a house on the outskirts of town, the home of a Colonel Fevzi. Dr. Adnan and the other deputies were whisked away to the men's quarters, where they were received by the colonel and his staff. Halide and I were taken to the harem. The colonel's wife was an ample figure, clad in old-fashioned pantaloons and waistcoat. The moment she laid eyes on us she threw back her veil, pattered across the room, grasped Halide with both hands, and kissed her cheeks. Halide was visibly startled, but once she had recovered she held the woman's face in her hands and wept. I shifted from one foot to the other wondering about the identity of this stranger who produced such violent emotion in my friend.

"Didar Hanim was the daughter of our neighbor in Sultantepe." Halide turned to me, her eyes moist. "She will be a thread to the past and it will be a great comfort having her close by."

"How long since you last saw one another?" I envied the closeness of her past, for mine became more remote as the days and weeks passed.

"At least twenty years; she knew my grandmother, and my father, and my poor stepmother Teyze, God rest her soul."

Didar Hanim gave me a hug. Her body was soft like a sponge, but her grasp was strong; her voice was forceful and as she spoke I was overwhelmed by the smell of garlic.

"Didar Hanim welcomes you, and is honored to have you as a guest in her home," translated Halide. I murmured a polite response, but then her face swam in front of my eyes and I forgot for a moment where I was and how I came to be there. As I struggled to bring myself back to the present, a serving girl entered carrying a samovar; others followed bearing trays of sweetmeats. The women spread a white cloth on the floor and laid out porcelain painted with flowers and edged in gold. One by one they placed the cups in the saucers and began pouring tea. Halide and Didar fell into conversation and no one appeared to have noticed my lapse.

Almost three weeks had passed since we left Istanbul.

"I must get word to the admiral that we are safe," I said. "My family will be desperate with worry. My sister is due any day now."

"We will try first thing tomorrow," said Halide. "The Farm School has its own switchboard."

I must have looked confused, for she put her hand on my arm in a conciliatory way.

"Didn't I tell you? Adnan and I have been given an apartment in the dormitories at the Agricultural College, where Mustafa Kemal has set up our headquarters."

"Am I to go with you?"

"Adnan and I thought you would be more comfortable with Miss Allen and Miss Billings, in the Christian quarter."

"They are here?" I said, cheering at the prospect of seeing Americans again.

"They're in Konya at the moment," she explained. "Mustafa Pasha has the keys. He will take you there any time you wish," she added.

"Surely the pasha is a busy man?" I said, affecting a casual indifference.

"Don't pretend with me — we know each other too well," said Halide laughing. "I've seen the way you look at one another, and then, when Mustafa came all the way to Lefke, I knew there was more to his feelings than simple Nationalist gratitude."

"I didn't want to distract you," I said, relieved she had not been deceived.

"Since I have devoted my soul to our struggle, the old Halide—the writer, mother and lover—has been suppressed, but she is not blind." My friend paused and looked around the room as if expecting to find someone listening, then turned her attention to me again and spoke in a conspiratorial whisper. "I have known passion and I know how rare it is."

That silhouetted figure we had seen in Camlica floated through my mind.

"After Mustafa's son died he became a new man, totally focused on our struggle as if he needed to justify his loss. He became devoted to Mustafa Kemal; but Kemal demands absolute loyalty from those around him."

"What are you telling me?"

"Be careful." She paused. "Kemal is fearless and unyielding."

"Neither of us expected to feel this way again, believe me, Halide."

"I believe you, but be careful," she repeated. I had the sense there was more she wanted to say, but she restrained herself.

Our carriage jolted back and forth across the road over potholes. Mustafa sat beside me, holding my hand in his lap. There was an awkwardness between us; something I could not define. His manner was distant yet loving, and I thought again what a mystery he was, for the closer we became the less I knew of him. Placing my hands on his cheeks, I turned his face toward me. His piercing eyes sent a tremor to my core, and I stopped myself from covering him with kisses.

As we entered the Christian quarter, mud houses gave way to stone villas, windows shuttered, doors barred and the gardens left to run wild. We clattered across a square and stopped in front of a double-fronted house surrounded by trees and bushes in need of pruning. A vine clambered over the façade, obscuring the windows and reaching to the tiles of the roof. At any moment the entire house might be suffocated with creeper and disappear in a barrage of foliage. How melancholy it seemed; I shivered as I pushed the gate open and hurried along the path.

The front door was ajar and I glanced around, taking in the bare floors and unexpected floral wallpaper peeling at the edges. Four rooms opened off the rectangular hall, each furnished with divans interspersed with European-style chairs and Turkish copper tables. Frayed lace curtains hung at the windows, yellowing from exposure to the sun. One room was lined with bookcases crammed with leather-bound volumes; above the fireplace hung a large gilded crucifix.

I said, "Who put that there?"

"The former inhabitants."

"Why did they leave their most valued possessions behind? Are they coming back?"

"In our struggle there is a place for those who prevaricate," he said, his tone suddenly harsh. That was the moment my unease started, like a small irritation that develops into a full rash. I turned away and walked into the kitchen. At the far end a capacious stone fireplace took up the length of one wall; to my right stood a pair of sinks with square wooden scrub boards, and in the center of the room was a table stacked with plates and dishes.

"They're porcelain," I exclaimed, running my fingers across the delicate china. "The last thing I expected to see in Anatolia."

"You will find every comfort here," said Mustafa.

"Where did this come from?"

"Miss Billings knows the details."

"When will they be back?"

"A week, a month, who knows. They are setting up an orphanage for the children of war victims." He moved closer and slipped his arm around my waist. "As long as Miss Billings and Miss Allen are in Konya I am free to remain here with you. But when they return it would not be proper, you understand?"

"I am plagued by the feeling my coming here has compromised you," I said, keeping my face turned away from him.

"Do not concern yourself with such foolishness. We both know the fleeting nature of life. Let us take what we can while we have it. I am answerable only to Mustafa Kemal, and he understands; he is a man of the world."

That night Mustafa and I lay together on the wide bed in a room overlooking the square. While he slept I watched the moon shadows flickering over the walls. How many years had passed since I lay with Burnham in this same trancelike state of happiness—two, three, no time at all. Dust caught in my throat, jerking me into a coughing fit; I sat up clutching my throat, but Mustafa did not stir. The covers rose and fell over his inert body while Burnham's ghost pushed through the walls. The scratch in my throat subsided. I fell on my pillow into a restless sleep until a crowing cock wrenched me into a new day. Mustafa was standing at the foot of the bed fully dressed save for the fez clutched in his hands.

"My colleagues will wonder what has become of me," he said abruptly.

"You are leaving so early?" I murmured, still drowsy from sleep.

"I have a long day ahead, Mary; we work from dawn to midnight. Mustafa Kemal never sleeps."

"Don't worry about me," I said, propping myself on my elbows, "I'm going to explore the town."

"When you leave the house wear the charshaf. I left it on the chair by the window."

"I thought your revolution was about progress. What is this practice of wrapping up your women?" I spoke too quickly, and he started as if I had slapped him.

"Anatolians are not accustomed to seeing foreigners in their streets, let alone a woman," he said sharply, clenching his fists as if to steady himself. "We are newcomers here. While some understand our mission, many remain suspicious. They are uneducated peasants who revere the sultan and the old ways. Help me, Mary; don't invite trouble."

"Annie and Florence go bare headed."

"They are known and beloved. Now I must go. The farm is half an hour from here. My comrades will wonder what has become of me."

"Mustafa."

"Yes?"

I reached out my hand toward him but a pained expression flickered across his face, and words of love faded from my lips. He hesitated, then leaned over and kissed my forehead.

I watched the soft mauve daylight break through the vines that crept over the window, not daring to think too far into the future. The charcoal and a drawing pad I had left behind at Rumeli Hisar Halide had thoughtfully stowed in my bag before we fled. If I sat in that bleak patch of mud and bushes Mustafa referred to as "the garden" I might find something of interest to draw.

The girl came soon after the sun reached mid-sky. She had a lazy eye that gave her the appearance of being lopsided. It was disconcerting to look at her. She put yogurt in a bowl with crumbled honeycomb and placed it on the dilapidated table in the back parlor that served as a dining room. While I ate I stared through the window at the castle rising in the distance.

After breakfast I wandered into one of the rooms overlooking the square and found a pile of books on a shelf behind the door. I brushed off the dust and read the titles: Victor Hugo, Voltaire and Emile Zola. Selecting a copy of Candide, I began to idly flip through the pages; the margins were filled with notes written in French in a small penciled hand. Certain words were underlined; sometimes entire passages were scribbled over two or three times. It began to dawn on me that this house had once belonged to Christians, Armenians or Greeks. I remembered Annie's words about the bloodshed that had torn apart the people of Anatolia.

The house took on a cold and unwelcoming aspect, and the book fell out of my hands. I sank to my knees, running my hand across the cover, going back over the confluence of accident and fate that had brought me this far. When Burnham died my life shattered into a thousand pieces, like a mirror dashed against a marble floor. Time passed, my life slowly came back together, but the fragmented glass had been rearranged, and the reflected image remained distorted. Gazing at myself, I wondered what had become of that woman I once knew.

Mustafa was elusive; there was something about him I did not understand. What did he want of me, and what was I looking for in him? Beset by these concerns, I put my sketchbook and charcoal into a bag, pulled the scarf over my head, and went out through the back door to see what I might discover about this unknown world.

The March air was cool, with a hint of spring. A large black bird flapped out of one of the trees and circled the square, cawing loudly as if to protest my intrusion. The neighboring villas were locked and shuttered, with no one about. Underfoot the cobbles became a mire of mud. I was about halfway along the alley, between high stone walls, when two women rounded the corner. The older carried a basket filled with vegetables, while the younger clutched a bundle of rags. Their faces were uncovered, with the same broad nose and sloping dark eyes ringed with kohl.

The moment they caught sight of me they froze and huddled close together. The conciliatory gesture I made only served to alarm them more; the younger one pulled her bundle close to her chest, while the other drew her scarf across the lower part of her face. As I walked toward them their eyes widened with fear. I smiled and bowed my head in greeting, and as I drew closer I was overcome by the strong smell of rose oil.

The women pressed themselves against the wall. I edged past, eyes down to avoid contact, but my curiosity got the better of me—I stole a glance at the bundle of rags and saw a tiny face concealed between the folds of dirty linen. It was an infant no more than two or three days old; the child's shriveled skin was white as alabaster, the eyes closed, the face so still I knew at once he or she was dead. A current of horror mingled with pity jarred my heart. I couldn't help thinking about Connie and her unborn child thousands of miles from this squalid alley.

The young mother paused to kiss the tiny face while the older woman looked on with such an expression of despair I scarcely know how to describe it. As they hurried on down the alley their robes swept against the ground, sending clouds of dust over the clumps of grass at the base of the wall. Was the baby recently dead? Where were they taking the body—to the cemetery? To their home? My head swirling with unanswered questions, I walked on blindly, oblivious to my surroundings, until I came across a low stone wall that enclosed a tidy orchard. I surmised this was the boundary of the mahalle, for beyond the orchard, brown fields stretched across a wide valley. I found a quiet spot where two walls intersected, affording protection from the wind.

Setting my bag on the ground, I removed my pad and charcoal and began drawing; one after the other, hasty sketches of the two women and their dead child, while the memory was painfully fresh.

Late in the afternoon Halide appeared at my door offering apologies for her unexpected intrusion. She shifted her gaze around the dark hallway and then settled her eyes on me.

"Mustafa Kemal has asked you to dine with us at the Farm School."

"Me? Why?" I said, amazed he even knew who I was.

"Without you there would be no Amasya accord."

"I am becoming embarrassed by that incident. I acted on the spur of the moment, nothing heroic. I didn't know a thing about your cause."

"We cannot waste the luxury of having an English speaker in our midst," said Halide. "You will also write dispatches for Admiral Bristol; he asked for reports on the progress of our struggle. He is a crucial ally; our information will go directly to the State Department."

I was taken aback. This was the same assignment Bristol had asked me to accept what seemed like an eternity ago.

"How will my letters reach him?"

"We have couriers who pass back and forth across the border under cover of night; this is how we stay in touch with our colleagues in Istanbul."

It was all deceptively simple—watch, listen, report what I saw, like letters sent from vacation in a wild, unusual place. Nothing more than the letters to our parents from the Grand Canyon and Utah that Burnham and I sent from our travels in the West.

Halide pressed her face against the window pane.

"Sun is starting to set; we must leave." She handed me a black scarf identical to the one she was wearing.

"Why do we have to be covered; who is going to see us in the dark?" I said, holding the scarf at arm's length.

"We are watched wherever we go. The locals are curious and suspicious; theirs are the hearts we have to win."

We passed an ancient aqueduct whose arches had collapsed leaving piles of stones on the ground, pocked with tufts of grass. On we went through a landscape of sloping brown fields, a glistening river meandering in the distance. From the fields arose a domelike phalanx topped with four ruined columns.

"Halide stop, I've never seen . . ." I said.

"Mausoleums for long forgotten saints, probably Christian," she said. "You'll see mounds just like it all over Anatolia."

"Could it be Byzantine?" I said, flattening my face against the window.

"Could be Roman. This land has been inhabited since time began," said Halide. "They are known only as remnants of *jahiliyya*, the godless era before Mohammed."

"Can we take an afternoon to walk around and explore the past?"

"The future is my concern; if there is to be one, you and I will be the origins," Halide replied enigmatically.

The hills gradually began to build one upon another, and the horses slowed. It was almost dusk by the time we reached the gates guarded by armed soldiers. Beeches lined the drive. Their branches swept almost to the ground like tiered crinolines. A low stone building came into view, half hidden behind banked acacias. This was the Farm School, the center of the Nationalist movement we had traveled so far to join. Pausing before the main door, I felt a twinge of doubt.

The atmosphere inside was austere, like a monastic order where the supplicants delivered themselves without question to the will of an imperious deity. Halide strode across the hall and through an open door into a long, narrow room, where the air smelled of stale smoke and the walls were yellow from age. In the center of the floor was a trestle table strewn with papers that almost buried a lone skeletal typewriter, pockmarked and with missing keys. Beside it was a basket covered with a red cloth that moved up and down of its own accord. Halide took hold of a corner and pulled it back to reveal five kittens.

"Their mother, Kadife Hanim, belongs to Dr. Refik; when these little ones were born he strung the room with red ribbons and handed out red sherbet. Our colleagues thought he was mad, but I understood. Motherhood must be honored in the traditional way."

A balding man came into the room and sat down in front of the ancient typewriter; I had seen him before on the train.

"You remember Yunus Nadi Bey," said Halide.

Nadi Bey gave me a terse nod.

"Together we are setting up a news agency to get word of our struggle out to the people."

"You have a printing press?" I exclaimed.

"Of course not. News of what is happening here in Angora and on the battle front will be sent over the wires, printed out at every town and village with a telegraph office, then posted on the wall of the local mosque, or in the office itself," said Halide. She picked up a yellowing copy of a French newspaper. "This way our people throughout Anatolia will be kept informed. Who knows, our news might even attract the attention of the outside world."

"What do you need with these French papers?"

"I must keep up with what they are saying about us. For this I'll need your help." She gave me a wry smile.

"My French is fragmented."

"No no no—your task will be to read the English papers, tell me everything they say, no matter how small or seemingly unimportant. We have to combat their prejudice. Time is our enemy. The Allies are working to impose their will on the sultan's government and compel them to sign a treaty that will be the death of this land."

A clanging bell signaled supper was about to be served. We joined a crowd of men who thronged into the main hall talking among themselves. One or two greeted Halide and cast me a look of passing curiosity. We were the only women present; even the servants were male. As we were about to enter the dining room I saw the back of Mustafa's head and hurried to catch up with him, but Halide caught hold of my arm.

"Stay with me," she whispered. "You will be seated together, but it is better not to speak to him now."

I sat between Halide and Mustafa at the horseshoe-shaped table, Adnan on her other side. Most of the forty or so men wore military uniforms that may have been patched and darned, but every one of them was meticulously groomed. Mustafa Kemal sat at the head of the table, immaculate in plus fours, striped shirt and tweed waistcoat. Seated at the far end of the table, more than a great revolutionary he reminded me of an English country gentleman. In repose his face was stern, but when he spoke his manner was intense. His listeners acquiesced before him; I understood at once he was a leader of uncommon strength.

Servants set out platters of rice and a meat stew swimming with vegetables. Mustafa inclined his head in a way to indicate I should serve him, but before doing that I heaped my own plate first. He caught my eye and frowned. I felt irritated by this change of manner. I had not come this far to be a servant. While we were eating he talked to his neighbor, a thin man with a livid scar running down his left cheek that gave his face a frightening demeanor. Though Mustafa did not touch liquor, his colleague consumed glass after glass of the cloudy alcohol the

Turks call raki, and their conversation escalated into a heated dialogue. No one paid me any attention. All around voices rose, while I ate in silence, acutely aware of my status as an interloper.

"Mustafa Kemal is to make an important announcement tonight," said Mustafa, finally turning back to me.

"I promise to listen very carefully. He has a strong face," I observed, studying Mustafa Kemal in repose. "Is he an easy man to work with?"

"We are united in our purpose; that is all that matters," replied Mustafa.

"But he is a soldier and you are a scholar."

"The perfect balance."

"Who is the leader?"

"I would follow the ghazi to the end of the earth," Mustafa replied, his gentle tone masking something hard and resolute. It made me wary; I had come this far because I cared deeply for this man, but his cause came between us like an invisible wall.

Mustafa Kemal banged the table with his fist, and the room fell silent. As he began reading from his sheaf of papers, an audible gasp of incredulity went around the table as if a thousand volts of electricity had been injected into the air. Halide reached for Adnan's hand. Mustafa sat motionless, staring straight ahead, apparently unmoved by Kemal's words. Plates were pushed aside; the men stopped eating and talked among themselves. Once Mustafa Kemal had finished he glared around the table. For a moment his eyes rested on me and hardened. I trembled. Never before had I felt such strength in a human face. If I hadn't been trembling so much I would have memorized his features, for he was a subject like no other.

"The Shey-Ul –Islam has issued a fatwa sentencing eight of us to death. We are at the top of their list along with Mustafa Kemal and his cabinet," whispered Halide.

"What does that mean?"

"It is the religious duty of all Muslims to kill us on sight."

"My God," I gasped.

"Our deaths will guarantee the killer a place in Paradise. Now we are a target for every religious fanatic from here to Erzerum."

"You knew, didn't you?" I whispered to Mustafa.

"Since this morning. Mustafa Kemal has already put his plan into action."

"What is Mustafa Kemal going to do?" I asked, reflecting on the dangerous position I now found myself in.

"The local people must not hear of this. Every newspaper from Istanbul will be seized at the border," whispered Mustafa. "Tomorrow we will counter this edict with our own fatwa from a sympathetic mufti."

"The sultan is becoming desperate," said Adnan, putting his arm around Halide. "This madness will sever the country, set brother against brother, and push the people into civil war."

"My poor sisters—how they will be suffering," Halide exclaimed. "I pray my boys do not get to hear of it."

"The school will protect your sons." Adnan drew her close, the first sign of physical affection I had witnessed between the two of them.

Mustafa talked animatedly with his colleagues. After the initial shock they seemed calm. Gradually the room filled with smoke, and my eyes stung. It must have been past midnight when Halide, who did not touch a drop of alcohol, tapped my shoulder and suggested it was time to leave. I whispered farewell to Mustafa. He squeezed my arm and nodded, but made no move to join me.

Halide and I linked arms and walked down the path leading to the stable yard. The night was cold, and a myriad of stars shimmered in the clear sky. The peace was suddenly broken by a deep and throaty barking.

"My loyal friend Karabash is doing her job," said Halide. "We will be safe tonight."

"Karabash?"

"My Anatolian sheepdog is unafraid of any danger," she said, stopping to look up at the sky. "Even though I have never had more reason to be afraid, I am filled with a sense of the fullness of this, our life."

"The stars do look particularly brilliant tonight," I murmured, gazing up at the sky dark as liquid velvet.

"'Oh raise me from the earth that from the heights I may look upon the world," said Halide. "My translation is inadequate. Persian is the language of the Sufi poets, the expression of the mystics; the original has greater force."

"Are the Sufis and the dervishes the same?" I asked.

"The two are like the threads on a loom," she replied. "Different colors, varying textures interwoven together to make a single carpet of immeasurable beauty."

# 23

I woke late the following morning, long after Mustafa had gone. Had he been there at all? Was this all a dream? Any moment I would wake and find myself back in my bed on Tenth Street preparing for another day at the Art Students League. The carriage had been waiting in the square for some hours. I dressed hastily and left without eating the meal the girl had prepared. By the time I reached the Farm School it was almost noon. As I entered the office I found Halide disconsolate, slumped in a chair, a letter on her lap. She stared vacantly at the window.

"The Allies have seized our home in Rumeli Hisar," she said in a flat voice. "I feared this day would come. A house is more than bricks and wood—it was our refuge. Now the enemy have taken that away from us."

Throwing my arms around her neck, I held her close, and for once she did not resist. Halide disliked outward displays of emotion; she buried her passionate nature so her mind might remain clear and directed.

"A refugee from Istanbul gave me this letter from Nighar." She held the paper close to her face and read aloud in halting English for my benefit. "'My dear sister, may Allah give you all health and safe passage. The fatwa is posted on every mosque and police station. It is the talk of the city. The people are with you, my beloved sister.

"'When we went to check on your beautiful, blessed home, it was surrounded by police. A hodja stood in the hall where you and I have greeted one another in happier times. He had the look of a man who hates women and beats his wife. As we came in, the fool brandished a bible in my face. "Look what we found in Halide Hanim's harem," he said. "She deserves to die for such blasphemy." I went to your room and fetched a Holy Koran. "My sister is a faithful Muslim, clean in her heart and soul," I said to the stupid, ignorant creature.

"'Nakiye Hanim was scolding a young policeman from the village for searching through the linen cupboard with dirty hands. God bless her courage. The boy went scarlet and offered to return everything they confiscated once the religious authorities had gone. I told him he was a coward for collaborating with the enemy. He begged my forgiveness. He was a poor boy just doing his job and supporting his widowed mother. Nakiye Hanim agonizes that you are criticizing her beloved sultan. I tried to explain he is a puppet in the hands of our enemies, but she asks how the infallible and great and mighty sultan can be anyone's puppet.'"

"You see what we are up against," said Halide, looking up at me over her glasses. "We are careful never to condemn the sultan. The masses revere him as God's representative on earth."

"If you are a faithful Muslim, Halide, is it easy for you to hear criticism?"

"The sultan has failed his responsibilities; our goal is to build democracy from the tenets of our faith. Our hope is that he will one day give us his blessing," she said slowly before turning her attention back to her sister's letter. "'The enmity toward the occupiers is growing with each day. Assassins killed Allied soldiers with knives concealed in their sleeves. An Englishman was stabbed on the Galata tram, just yesterday.

"'Do not worry about your boys. We went to visit them at the American School after Friday prayers. Their health and outlook are positive; they know nothing of the fatwa. They share a room facing the water and are studying hard for their exams. Merciful Allah has answered your prayers, sweet sister. Mr. Charles Crane will transport them to live with his family in Chicago; the money you provided will pay for their education! We rejoiced with them. They will leave next month. Never fear, my sister — they will be safe from physical harm, but I trust you know what you are doing sending them so far from their family and the place of their birth. Mr. Crane assures you he will write to you through the American consul.'"

Halide leaned back and let her arms drop to her sides.

"To survive I have to put the past out of my mind," Halide said, "and forget the world as it was, for those times will never return. My sons are modern boys; this sacrifice is for their future."

Two days later, on April 23, the Grand National Assembly officially convened in Angora. Mustafa Kemal had deliberately chosen Friday, the Muslim day of prayer, to open the new and hopeful legislative body of the people. In the days prior to the inauguration, Mustafa crafted a revised draft of the historic speech Kemal would deliver to the assembly.

Kemal, the consummate soldier, relied on Mustafa, the poetic intellectual, to galvanize the spirit of his people. Mustafa did not sleep and ate only when I reminded him. He roamed through the house at night murmuring to himself, slamming the walls with his palm when an auspicious idea came to him and with equal force when a phrase eluded him. Papers littered the rooms, covered in his flawless script. I concealed one of his discarded manuscripts at the bottom of my bag. The Arabic letters were a work of art, something akin to sacred. I have kept them to this day.

It goes without saying that as a nonbeliever and a woman, I did not attend the ceremony that began at the Haci Bayram Mosque beside the tomb of the town's favorite saint. To combat the charges that they were godless nonbelievers, the Nationalists included recitations from the Koran, and they sacrificed a hapless sheep, a ritual Halide deplored. Prayers were offered for the sultan caliph's safety, and a hair from the Prophet's beard was displayed and venerated. An imam bearing the standard of the Prophet led the procession to the parliament building. The proceedings were duly reported to Admiral Bristol in my daily dispatch, albeit secondhand and with some editing.

My correspondence with the consulate was a one-way affair; messages from Admiral Bristol were oblique and at best occasional. The admiral was known to be a copious correspondent, meticulous about detail; it was obvious his responses were being intercepted by the Allied censors. It was hard knowing nothing about my family. Not a day passed when I didn't think of them.

I found solace in my work. My sketchbook was soon filled and I made do with the backs of used envelopes and discarded telegrams. I kept everything, for I sensed denouement was at hand. I was an artist, not a politician; although I felt strong sympathy for the struggle, I did not grasp its subleties. Even the language eluded me. How could I be part of this world if I could not communicate? As winter faded and the dark hills around the Farm School turned a miraculous green, something inside me shifted, and I knew I could not live this way much longer.

During the first week of April, Karabash disappeared. Halide was distraught. Her beloved dog was her friend, at her side protecting her while she rode in the afternoon, at the gate every night, one ear cocked for the sound of enemy footfall. Now that enemy was moving closer; news reached us that caliphate sympathizers had been discovered in the old town. We searched for Karabash in the fields, in the valley, and on the wooded hillside above the house but found nothing. Knowing the faithful animal would never wander far from her side, Halide was forced to admit he was probably dead; we held a prayer vigil in the meadows beside the stream where he once played in the long grass.

Pain shot down my back and through every muscle and crevice in my shoulders; I reached forward and yanked the paper from the typewriter. It had taken almost two hours to type a single page on the Underwood Zephyr. Halide and I wrestled with this recalcitrant typewriter during the day, Nadi Bey at night. He was a newspaperman accustomed to working late hours, and sometimes when I arrived he was still bent over the keys muttering to himself as he hammered away.

The nape of my neck was damp with perspiration; I twisted my hair into a knot and fastened it with a beech twig. May was nearly over, and we were feeling the first hint of the intense Anatolian summer. Our one window opened onto an enclosed courtyard; circulation was poor and the air stood stagnant for hours. Sometimes when we were alone, Halide and I, like mischievous sorority girls, closed the door, removed our scarves, and let our hair fall free down our backs.

The bell clanged down the corridor. After wiping my ink-stained hands, I retrieved my scarf from the floor where I had tossed it in a fit of resentment. I was alone in the office. Halide had one of her regular meetings with Mustafa Kemal, and Yunus Bey was asleep in his room after working through the night. Pushing every hair out of sight, I fastened the scarf and unlocked the door. Mustafa stood before me, his arms outstretched. He must have run all the way from his office.

His study was situated at the far end of the building, on a corner, with windows that faced the gentle brown hills and meandering river. The town of Angora, with its distinctive hill and citadel, shimmered in the distance as mystical cities of the Italian Renaissance are recumbent in the background of Madonnas and nativities. Here Mustafa worked day after day, interpreting European political codes to the needs of the Nationalist government. He was scrupulous in his attention to detail and maintaining the legality of every change; for theirs was a government that rose from the will of people chafing under foreign occupation. Not for them the fate of India and Egypt; they all believed death was preferable to colonization. Mustafa waxed lyrical in his defiance, but his determination was as hard as the citadel stone.

Something was changed in his face; I saw it at once. He caught my arm and drew me close. His usual circumspect behavior around his colleagues was ignored. Now he seemed not to care. He held my arm and led me toward the door, whispering that we were to return to the house at once. He had sent word to the girl to leave food in the pantry by the back door. The bell ceased, and the last stragglers dashed past. Mustafa Kemal ran the headquarters with military precision, and tardiness was looked on as a serious breach.

Mustafa and I emerged into the warm air. Before us the beeches were bathed in the soft pink light of the dying sun, and the roofs of the outbuildings shone bronze. The wind had died and nothing stirred. We paused on the step and breathed the sweet smell of jasmine. The blur of white made me suddenly think of the garden beside Grace Church, where the daffodils would be full and gold, the last of the primroses bursting on the old graves at the back of the nave. Pain squeezed the pit of my stomach, and a sudden longing for the familiar steeple and carved doorways forced me to turn away lest Mustafa see my tears.

He touched my shoulder, then started along the path toward the stables. I followed after him, pulling the lower half of my scarf over my face as he preferred when we were together. I had become part of his world; every night we stayed together in the house as man and wife. In a few short weeks we had become physically inseparable.

As soon as we turned into the lane he leaned across the carriage and took my hands in his.

"The moment we dreaded has come," he said quietly. "We received reports the sultan's army is close to Ismidt, a few miles from here. I remember their leader from the time of the Great War, an illiterate thug named Anzavour. Mustafa Kemal has ordered Ali Fuad Pasha to lead our forces against him. I will go with them."

Beads of sweat swelled at his hairline. As I brushed them away with the back of my hand, he caught my wrist. Cupping my face in his hands, he drew me so close that I saw his eyes were crisscrossed with blood-red veins.

"The path to our goal has become clouded by civil war; I cannot sit here and watch while others fight and die on the battlefield."

"When do you leave?" Struggling to stay calm, I closed my eyes.

"Tomorrow, at sunrise."

A familiar dread clogged my chest; I remembered another farewell, on a windy quay in Brooklyn. Since that fateful morning it seemed an eternity had passed.

"I have been down this road before, Mustafa."

"What can I say?"

"Nothing, nothing; you must leave."

"Our happiness was fleeting, but we have been blessed." With a look that spoke anguish, he relinquished his hold and helped me into the waiting carriage. Once we were settled, he thrust his head and shoulders through the open window and called out to the driver.

Behind the horizon the sun sank in a blaze of red, and clouds tinged with pink turned gray. Just as we reached the place where the lane divided, our carriage swung to the left, away from town.

"He's going the wrong way," I said.

"You always wanted to explore that ancient mausoleum."

"It's almost dark."

"I brought lamps; they are up front with the driver."

"Lamps?"

"I want you to remember me well when I am gone."

Darkness came quietly, and all that remained of this last sunset was a faint band of gold along the horizon. Clutching his arm, I walked gingerly across the plowed earth, taking care to keep within the beam of light thrown by the lantern. The ground was littered with pointed stones that poked through the soil like a thousand spearheads stabbing at the soles of my boots.

"Once upon a time there was a settlement here," Mustafa said, kicking at the soil, scattering it to reveal an odd-shaped stone about six inches long.

"Wait, what's this?" I got down on my knees to take a closer look. Holding it high between thumb and forefinger, I saw it was a piece of pottery, brown with wavy lines incised on the outer shell.

"These remnants are everywhere," said Mustafa. "I have found whole plates, some with nothing more than a chip."

"I will keep this forever." I tucked the shard into my pocket and hurried after him.

The foot of the mound was steeper than it appeared from the lane; the ground was covered with grass and wildflowers. I could not see a path, so I followed him through the damp grass until we had almost reached the summit. Then he paused to look back. The air had cooled and mist cloaked the countryside, obscuring the distant hills and the citadel of Angora. The moon was rising, almost full, and the bright aura glowed in the foggy night.

Up close the stones were massive and towered over us four times the height of a man. No markings or carvings gave a clue to their origin; it was as if some giant hand had plucked them from a distant quarry and set them on this man-made hill like candles on a birthday cake. They cast thick shadows across the grass, which was covered with a primrose-like flower, closed now that night had come. Mustafa and I leaned against a stone slab half buried in the ground, and he held the lamp high so I could survey the ruins. There was no sign of a tomb, or a sarcophagus, or a hidden door that might lead to a crypt deep underground. It occurred to me that this was not a mausoleum after all but a testimony to existence.

I rested the back of my head on his shoulder and closed my eyes, holding the moment. The memory of our intimacy would stay with me in the long days to come. He spread his coat on the ground beside one of the great stones; when we lay down I felt the cool earth pressing through my clothes. I ran my hands over his shoulder, through his hair, across his face, memorizing every inch of his body. We kissed like children snatching at candy, greedy for the taste of each other's mouth and lips. The knowledge of our imminent parting made us desperate. We clawed at one another, grasping, biting, until we were spent. Yet even in those anguished final moments I sensed his mind shifting to the fight ahead. We fell back in a tangled embrace and stared up at the spectacle of the vast unending universe.

"I don't care how long you will be gone; I'll wait for you," I whispered. He shifted on to his back; I could just make out his profile against the night sky. "Talk to me, Mustafa; say something."

"Words cannot adequately express the turmoil of the human heart," he sighed, pushing himself up on his elbows.

"You're not going to die, not yet. I know it."

"Ah, your premonitions," he said gently.

"We have many years ahead of us."

"My dear Mary. What can I offer here—hardship, uncertainty. You see how we live, stripped of luxuries like monks in a monastery."

"I am not a delicate woman who needs a silk cushion beneath her head every night."

"There is danger everywhere in Anatolia. Remember there is a warrant out for your arrest. If you return to the safety of your homeland you can still work for our cause, writing, lecturing, telling your people about the justice of our revolution."

"How can I return to America without passing through occupied territory?"

"No one knows what you look like; it would be an easy matter to smuggle you into the city."

An uneasy feeling communicated itself to me.

"You have thought about this."

"If anything happened to you I would never forgive myself."

"I can look after myself."

"We have no voice in America; you are the ideal person to tell your people about the justice of our cause."

"We might never see one another again."

He stroked my head. "Your warmth, your courage—coming here has given me the strength to move forward. You have no idea what a solace you have been these past few weeks, but our struggle demands total sacrifice."

"I can't leave you," I whispered, stroking his face with my fingertips.

"Go home to the protection of your family. Then I will rest easy knowing you are safe."

"I don't know where home is any more," I whispered.

"You will be in my heart until my dying breath."

"Don't talk of death, I beg of you."

Did he hear me? I don't know. He was already on his feet, brushing dirt from his coat. His body radiated the restlessness I had come to recognize when he was preoccupied. His mind was already roaming the steppes. It was time to leave, to descend the hill, to climb into the carriage and return to town. I straightened my clothes, brushed the grass from my hair, and pulled the scarf close around my shoulders. Determined that I would not give way to tears, I savored our final moments together, impressing them in my memory to hold through the long days ahead.

# 24

I lay awake staring at the dark stains on the ceiling, which were spreading like a canker. There was a faint dank odor, and I wondered how long it would be before the smell became unbearable. Six weeks had passed since Mustafa had left for Ismidt. To mask his absence I had created a new routine. During the day I ventured with my pad and charcoal into the old town, where I made sketches of local people, now visibly suffering the effects of hunger and deprivation, into the late afternoon. Never in my life had I lived in such a heady atmosphere of tension and danger. The unexpected consequence was that my drawing style became bolder. I harbored the fanciful notion their determination permeated my working mind. In the late afternoon I walked through the open meadows, past turrets of mist hovering above the river. At this time of year the drive leading to headquarters was covered with yellow-brown leaves. When Halide returned from her afternoon ride, the two of us spent the rest of the day composing dispatches for the English-language papers and daily letters for Admiral Bristol.

News from Ismidt was good. The young commander, Ali Fuad Pasha, had driven back the caliphate forces. No sooner had we rejoiced at this than word came of an uprising to the north where more forces

221

allied with the sultan. It was the beginning of the Safranbolu uprising, which soon spread to the Turkish areas around Angora. I heard Mustafa had moved north with a band of independent fighters, but concrete information was scant.

Meanwhile, in the West, Greek troops were pressing inland from Smyrna; Cilicia was held by the French. In the occupied territory the Allies maintained their control with an iron fist. Surrounded by enemies, the Nationalists' mood remained buoyant. Although I missed Mustafa, working with his colleagues carried me through those long days.

While I was dressing, the front door slammed. Startled from my reverie, I ran to the landing and peered over the banister in time to see Florence Billings walk into the hall, sagging under the weight of a large box.

"Florence," I cried, starting down the stairs two at a time, "what are you doing here?"

"We had to flee Konya under cover of darkness and drove all night." She set the box on the floor. "Fighting broke out all over the town. Annie and I were trapped in the orphanage. I didn't think we'd get out alive."

"Rest, Billy, you sound exhausted."

"Our workload has increased tenfold. We scarcely had time to sleep or eat. The situation in Anatolia has become nightmarish." There was no trace of self-pity in her voice. "Thank goodness you are here, Mary. God answered my prayers."

At that moment Annie Allen appeared in the doorway clutching a basket to her chest. Her clothes hung loose from bony shoulders, her cheeks had hollowed, and there were dark rings around her eyes. The change in her appearance was startling. I took a sharp breath and tried to disguise my shock.

"Mary, you are a welcome sight," said Annie. As she set the basket on the floor I saw that her hands were shaking. "I just learned of your escape when I was in Istanbul."

"When were you there?"

"I returned ten days ago, before the fighting worsened; I did not want to risk sending a letter to Mark Bristol, so I decided to go in person."

"What is the problem with a letter?" I said to her.

"Your letters have been invaluable. Mark made a point of telling me how grateful he was for your information. The situation is changing fast—the civil war is escalating and the Greeks are moving inland on their foolhardy mission to restore the glory of Byzantium."

"And the countryside is overrun with disease," said Florence, smiling at Annie. "Rest, we have Mary to help us, and the men."

A breeze swept through the hall carrying twigs and dry leaves from the garden; they whirled in a circle and settled on the wooden floor.

At the end of the path, beyond the wall, a crowd of men stared at the car with unalloyed curiosity. Some ran their fingers through the dust coating the chassis, others stroked the steering wheel as if feeling the coat of a fine horse. Ignoring Florence's admonition, Annie walked down the path, moving with the hobbled gait of an invalid; she waved aside my offer to help her with a brusque "I can manage."

The moment the men saw her they scooped their fezzes from their heads and clutched them to their chests. Annie acknowledged them with a smile and began searching through the boxes piled in the back seat of the car.

"Where are those extra bandages, Billy? I thought we packed them with the blankets."

"Bandages are in short supply. Why do you need them now?"

"Just look at these poor souls. They have only dirty rags tied around their wounds."

"We have sick children to care for. We can't go handing out our supplies to everyone who comes begging. Besides, these men are war veterans, supposedly under the care of Mustafa Kemal," Florence protested.

"When I meet with the pasha I will remind him of his responsibilities; in the meantime it is our duty to help everyone in need."

Annie stood straight, one hand on the car chassis, and started talking to the men. Her shoulders heaved and her words came slowly; the effort of speech was apparent. On the faces of those men I saw such pathos, their gaunt eyes widened as if she was their last hope.

"What happened?" I whispered to Florence.

"Typhoid, there was an outbreak in Konya; it's all over Anatolia. Our little hospital was flooded with victims. We worked night and day. It was inevitable one of us would succumb. Then no sooner than she recovered, Annie insisted on going to Istanbul to see Mark Bristol. That trip set her back."

"How did you avoid getting sick?"

"My years on the battlefields in France have given me immunity." Her eyes took on a fleeting expression of sadness; it flashed, and vanished, like a reflection of a bird flying over a stream.

Annie swayed, put her hand against the car and slumped forward. The men backed away, reluctant to touch a woman. Florence and I rushed to her side and caught hold of her arms to prevent a fall. Her bones felt like twigs, light and airy, as if the weight of human concern had already departed, leaving only the spirit contained in her skeletal frame. We carried her inside and laid her on the sofa in the drawing room at the front of the house. Florence threw her shawl over Annie's inert body and placed a pillow under her head.

"I'll be fine," Annie whispered. "Please let me alone."

"Give me your word you will not move. I don't have time to take care of one more sick person."

Annie was too weak to give anything more than an assenting nod.

Florence and I worked all day unloading the car and organizing the house until the dining room was transformed into an office with a modern typewriter, papers, pens and leather-bound ledgers. I don't know how Florence found time to keep a record of their days in her meticulous copperplate script. The wide hall became a dispensary, with white metal bowls and strange-looking medical utensils lined in neat rows across the old table. Boxes of unused bandages were ranged along the back wall under a shelf of medication in amber-colored bottles. When all was in place the sense of accomplishment gave me quiet peace. The simple physical work provided relief from my teeming mind.

"Unless Annie rests she will kill herself." Florence said looking up at me. We were scrubbing the kitchen table; my eyes burned from the bleach. "Don't look alarmed, she's asleep, she can't hear me. Anyway she knows what I think about her pushing herself too hard."

"We never believe we will die."

"She would risk her life for these people. She understands how they have suffered better than any diplomat or politician in Paris or Istanbul. The end of the war has brought chaos. There are discharged soldiers armed and destitute roaming all over the countryside. Some fight for the Nationalists, some for the sultan, most would kill for a loaf of bread. It's a tinderbox, Mary. Do you really understand what you have walked into?"

Her question was unexpected. Not knowing how to answer, I looked down and starting scrubbing with renewed vigor.

"Understanding or not, I thank God you are here. At dawn tomorrow you and I will go to the orphanage. Annie will stay here. I dread to think how many desperate people will be waiting. Exposing herself to more disease will be the worst thing she can do."

Wiping her hand across her eyes, I noticed her tapered fingers and narrow wrist, white and unmarked.

"Oh, I nearly forgot. Mark Bristol sent some letters for you. Annie carried them from Istanbul. They are in the trunk at the foot of the stairs."

The package was surprisingly large. It was tied like a parcel, the knot sealed with red wax stamped with the consulate eagle. Most of the letters were addressed in Connie's round, extravagant hand; my heart trembled at the sight of them. There was one I did not recognize. The envelope was cream vellum, with my name typed in capital letters and no return address. Florence insisted I read them in the garden, away from the blistering smell of bleach.

Outside the light was starting to fade, the air had cooled, and a faint haze shimmered above the wall, giving the fortress the appearance of floating above the town. The sight released in me a wave of feeling. This barren landscape was becoming familiar, working its way into my heart like a burrowing animal. There was a bench beneath the fig tree. I opened the first of Connie's letters.

"Dearest Mary," she wrote, "George Henry Olsen was born on March 22nd, two weeks early, but don't worry, we are both in good health. He has John's blue eyes and a patch of sandy hair. George is the most beautiful person I have seen in my life. Even the nurse comments how good he is. I hover over the cradle waiting for his eyes to open so he knows I am there. He knows me now. Dear God, how is it possible to love another human being the way I love him? He is the center of our life. I wish you were here to share this joy with us.

"John's health is improving, and the birth of his son has done wonders; he is very very proud. Every afternoon John joins Nanny and me as we walk to Washington Square and back. This week I plan to stop in at the Macbeth Gallery. Two months have passed since we took your paintings there. I'm sorry, I have been so preoccupied I have not had time to talk to them. Admiral Bristol promises to send these letters on. I pray they are reaching you. Please know we are thinking about you all the time, wondering and worrying. If you can drop me a note, a letter, anything to let us know you are safe. Your loving sister, Connie."

With care I folded the letter into a square and tucked it back in the envelope. Spreading my palm, I held my hand above my head and let the wind rush through my fingers. The loving sister in me would write, expressing joy for the birth of my nephew, assuring them I was safe, even happy. Conveying a truer state of mind was impossible. I didn't know myself.

The bundled letters slipped off my lap and scattered on the ground; I picked up the cream vellum note card.

"Dear Mrs. Di Benedetti, I am pleased to inform you that you have been formally pardoned by the Allied Commander, General Milne. An order to that effect is being distributed immediately to all Allied forces throughout the Ottoman territories. The situation in Anatolia is perilous, civil war looms, and a Greek invasion is expected any day now. I am about to leave for a reconnaissance in the Nationalist zone and will be in Angora toward the end of May. At that time Admiral Bristol and I recommend you return with me to Istanbul. Your work is done; you have been an invaluable observer. Yours, Robert Dunn, Lieutenant."

To make sure I grasped his meaning, I read the letter twice. "Your work is done." What presumption! The observations and ideas experienced in my day-to-day life had nothing to do with Robert Dunn. Those reports were nothing more than detailed letters to a friend describing daily life in Angora, letters written with the full assent of Halide and her colleagues so the world might understand the seriousness of their cause. Now a professional intelligence officer shattered those illusions. How naïve that sounds! I was a spy whose tour was over; my usefulness had become an embarrassment. My hands fell into my lap as I struggled to come to grips with this discomforting revelation.

It crossed my mind the warrant might have been nothing more than an empty threat concocted by the Allies to warn American sympathizers, of whom there were many among the community in Istanbul. Why had it taken me so long to understand that my position as sister-in-law, widow of a war hero, and American citizen set me apart from my new friends.

Somewhere between my arrival on that cold February morning and this moment in a remote corner of Angora the affections and loyalties in my heart had shifted. We Americans had no sympathy for imperialist ambition, and the old prewar attitudes of cultural superiority and the right to occupy were on the brink of extinction, but the Allies did not yet understand. Taking the vellum between my fingers, I tore the letter into small pieces and threw them in the air. They floated to the ground like confetti tossed at a wedding.

# 25

The following morning I was woken by the sound of raised voices and crying babies; I walked over to the window. Below me, in the street, a line of women and children stretched from the gate to the corner. Some lay in the dirt, heads propped against makeshift pillows, others leaned against the garden wall, knees drawn to their chins. Most stood talking in groups. Babies clung to their mothers' breasts while older children played in the dirt or held tightly to women's skirts. As I parted the curtain to look out, heads swiveled and anxious faces turned upward. It was barely light; the ragged procession must have arrived before dawn. From the direction of town came the cry of a muezzin, the first call to prayer.

It was a welcome sound marking the arrival of a new day. I remembered there were friends in the house; I was no longer alone, and for the first time in weeks I felt a surge of happiness. In this mood of new joy I made my way downstairs, where, to my surprise, I found Halide in the kitchen stirring a cauldron of rice bubbling in the fireplace. Florence was ladling yogurt out of a large urn into cracked china bowls on the table.

"The cook at headquarters was told by his brother that Florence and Annie arrived from Konya," said Halide. "I came at once."

"No secrets around here," said Florence, giving me a meaningful look. Unbidden the color rose in my cheeks; was Mustafa to be a subject of contention between us?

"As soon as the rice is cooked we will unlock the gate," said Halide. "They can eat in here; it is warm; the children can sit by the fire."

"I underestimated the numbers. I hope we have enough bowls," said Florence.

"We will make do," I said, stepping into the room. "As soon as the women are finished I will wash the dishes and make them ready for reuse."

"That's the spirit," said Florence.

I glanced around. There was no sign of Annie.

"Sleeping," said Florence as if reading my mind.

I still retain the image of scrawny children, noses running, with sticky fingers clutching spoons like shovels. Their ragged mothers, eyes ringed with fatigue, wandered in looking bowed and dazed. One by one they streamed into the kitchen trailing a faint odor of urine and sweat. While Halide ladled the rice and beans, I scooped up dishes and cleaned them in hot water boiled in the fireplace. All the while Florence tended the sick. She bandaged gaping wounds, cleaned scratches, searched scalps for traces of lice. When the ailment was serious she administered pills. She helped the weaker women onto the makeshift beds, where they stayed for several days.

We worked without stopping. Morning bled into afternoon, when an interval of silence descended. The food was finished, and most of the women began to drift away, trailing their children behind them. Heads bowed, they murmured quiet gratitude; few smiled. I have a memory of dark eyes brimming with tears and children clutching the last of the flatbread, fingers clenched around the crust as if it were made of gold. Hard physical work brought an unexpected lightness and left no time for contemplation. All the tangled thoughts of Mustafa, my pardon, and the impending arrival of Robert Dunn evaporated like water poured on hot stones.

Close to dusk Halide came into the garden. I had retreated to the stone bench beneath the fig tree where I customarily sat at the end of a long day watching the light change.

"I heard your news," she said quietly. "I am relieved you are no longer under the shadow of an Allied warrant, but the thought of losing you is very distressing. "

"I am not certain I am leaving, Halide. For all I know this could be an elaborate trap."

"Intuition tells me the Allies would never deliberately deceive Mark Bristol."

"Why have they suddenly put their suspicions aside and given me a pardon? It doesn't make sense. You said yourself the Allies have always known I took the papers from Halil and passed them on to you but could never prove it."

"Bristol is a brilliant diplomat, very persuasive. Who's that commander he is close to?"

"Heathcote Smythe?"

"Months passed and the furor over the papers subsided. Other issues became important, and then quietly, over a whisky or two, Bristol persuaded his friend to withdraw the warrant."

"Maybe," I said. "Sometimes I wonder if it was all a ruse from the start."

"Don't try to second guess their motives, Mary. The point is, you are now free to return to Istanbul."

"I'm not sure I wish to return."

"Don't let your feelings for Mustafa Pasha override common sense."

I can still recall the scolding edge to her voice. I had to remind myself there was another Halide, Corporal Halide, the soldier in the Nationalist army, for whom all emotional ties were suppressed in the cause of freedom.

"I have come to understand we do not have a future," I said, to placate her.

"The Greeks are moving inland. Who knows how long it will be before they reach the walls of Angora. I cannot be responsible for your safety."

"I am my own keeper. Besides, who will write the news for foreign papers?"

"I am fluent in English and French."

"You have enough to do," I said in what I hoped was a calm voice.

"If you leave with Dunn we will see one another again. I have promised myself I will come to America to see my boys." Her voice became a whisper. "When this war ends my dream is to be our first ambassador to the United States."

"But you're a woman," I said, remembering the table full of men with whom she sat night after night, debating the future.

"There is no one better qualified. Not one of those men has anywhere near my fluency in English. Don't breathe a word, Mary Hanim—not even Adnan knows; he disapproves of personal ambition. Our cause is for the collective good."

We sat in silence. Overhead the sky slid from blue to azure; another evening was beginning.

Just after dawn I was awake, disturbed by a cock crowing in a neighboring farmyard. I happened to look out of my window and saw a young man running across the square. From his khaki coat I took him to be a soldier, but his clothes were tattered, his boots scuffed, and despite the cold weather he did not wear a hat. He reached our gate, paused, and glanced up at the house. When he saw me, he raised his hand and beckoned. Strangers were regarded with caution, so I grabbed a sturdy walking stick before opening the door a crack.

"Good day, Madame, forgive the intrusion," he said in impeccable French. His narrow face was weather-beaten and patches of red flared under his eyes.

"What do you want here?"

"I have been sent by Mustafa Pasha."

The sound of his name sent my heart racing, but I hesitated, fearing a trick.

"Peace be with you," he murmured in broken English. This was the password Mustafa and I had agreed upon before he left.

"Come in, come in," I said, pulling wide the door.

"Thank you, but no," he resumed in French. "I am expected at headquarters; before reporting to my commanders I have to deliver a letter addressed to Madame Mary."

"That's me," I said. "So he is safe?"

"I am the messenger, Madame." With the barest of nods he handed me a scroll of paper and hurried away. Clutching the scroll to my chest, I watched until he disappeared around the corner of the square.

Even now, almost forty years later, I recall my intense feelings of excitement mixed with terror as I broke the wax seal and slowly unrolled Mustafa's letter, written in that perfect hand I first encountered in those mysterious manuscripts many months before. The hall was dark, so I made my way into the kitchen, where daylight filtered through the window overlooking the garden.

"My Dear," he wrote, "my dear I think of you constantly, at night as I fall asleep, in the morning when I wake. The memory of your love never leaves me until I force myself to look away and face the road ahead.

I cannot tell you where we are, save the enemy is close. By the time this letter is in your hands the battle will have begun. This opportunity to write may not come again, so I am telling you my feelings are as powerful as ever and will remain through eternity." No signature identified the writer, but I knew it was Mustafa.

The house was quiet; the silence pushed against me. I sat at the kitchen table, my elbows resting on the harsh wood, hands clasped in front of of me. The news he had reached the field of battle made me resolute and calm, as if a stream of hot iron flowed through my spine reaching every tip of bone, every nerve, until the cool spirit of purpose hardened. The sensation was familiar, like the face of an old friend seen in a crowd of strangers. I resolved to follow my instincts and ignore the quieter voice of reason; my heart was in Anatolia and nothing could tear me away. America was a country remembered in a dream, and the city where I was born forever changed by another loss in another time. I was young; thirty, forty years of life lay ahead, and I could not spend them filled with regret.

That night was to have been my last. Robert Dunn was in Angora. Although we had not yet spoken, word came from headquarters that he expected to meet with me the following morning in the office of Anatolian News.

I did my best to make the dining room look festive. In lieu of a cloth, a clean sheet covered the table, and cotton scarves served as napkins. For want of a candelabra I stuck candles into old flower pots secured by packed earth, like wax plants. Flowers were not a problem—they grew wild in the garden. I cut branches from the jasmine tree and stuck them in the pots. To this day the perfume reminds me of that night, when the still Angora air hung heavy with jasmine and the smell of burning wicks. Food was simple. I was not a good cook, and the girl who did the cleaning had a repertoire limited to rice and eggplant. Florence and Annie offered to help but I refused; this was to be my farewell.

Four charcoal drawings lay on the table, one for each of my guests — after Mustafa, my closest friends: Florence, Annie, Halide, and Adnan. Four dark, unsparing portraits of the mother and daughter with their dead child.

"This says it all," said Adnan holding his drawing at arm's length to see it without his glasses. "You have understood the spirit of our struggle, Mary. The curve of the mouth, the withered hand belying her age. The grandmother was probably no more than thirty. In the countryside girls are married off at a young age. "

"Then they die young in childbirth," said Annie, her face haggard even in the forgiving candlelight.

"Where is Robert Dunn tonight? Why didn't you invite him to join us, Mary?" said Florence, giving me an impish smile. "We need an extra man. Adnan is outnumbered."

"Dunn is meeting with Mustafa Kemal as we speak. A triumph for Bristol; my communiqués were diffuse by necessity," I replied.

"Indeed?" Adnan started, visibly surprised.

"I thought you knew," said Halide.

"Why didn't Kemal ask you to translate, my dear? "

"Dunn fancies himself fluent in Turkish."

"You have doubts?" I asked.

"Dunn speaks Turkish, but his understanding is limited," said Annie, her voice so weak we had to strain to hear her.

"Mustafa Kemal will confine himself to facts," said Halide. "Kemal wants America to understand the justice of our cause, nothing more. When he wants something he can be a plain-speaking man; his philosophical ramblings are usually reserved for his supporters."

"This is not the time to talk of Kemal," said Adnan. "Let's raise our glasses to friendship and shared ideals. Life is fragile, and we do not know when we will all meet again. This moment must be savored."

Before I could say another word, Halide scrambled to her feet and curled her arm around my neck, startling me with an overt display of affection.

"We will miss you," she murmured. "Mere words cannot convey how I will miss our conversations about art, literature, and New York."

"But I am NOT leaving," I blurted, my face flushed. This was not the way I planned to make my announcement. "I am staying. Perhaps not forever, but for now, while there is so much to be done." I turned to meet Halide's eye. "I want nothing more than to help relieve the suffering I see around me. I cannot just walk away. If Annie and Florence agree I want to stay, work with them. Even in the poorest neighborhoods of New York I have never seen a mother carrying her dead child through the streets of town without a hospital or doctor to tend her. That encounter put me on another road."

Only Florence was smiling.

So I remained in Anatolia, working in an unofficial capacity for Near Eastern Relief alongside Florence and Annie, who became colleagues, and in the case of Florence, a lifelong friend. Mark Bristol's response to my decision was sanguine. My refusal to return to Istanbul had caused some embarrassment with his Allied colleagues—after granting me a pardon to have it refused amounted to an insult. Mark understood that my experience in Anatolia had changed me. I was no longer a "civilian," to use his words. Halide, Adnan, and Mustafa lived for a cause greater than themselves. It was inevitable I would be influenced by their idealism. Bristol hinted I might still be of use, and I readily agreed. I wanted the truth to reach America

Using the diplomatic pouch, I sent word to my family; weeks passed before a response came, first from my parents, who were relieved I was working with American missionaries. Three months later I heard from Connie and John, who reminded me I was welcome in Washington where they now lived with their son. It would be many years before I returned to America and learned they had come to admire my decision.

Soon after the letter from Mustafa arrived I learned the "enemy" he referred to was the Greek army. Sometime in the new year they ambushed the Nationalist forces near the small town of Inonu, where Mustafa had been sent to serve with Kemal's colleague Colonel Ismet. Camped near the railway station, the Turks held off their attackers, waiting for backup forces to arrive. Then the Greeks suddenly retreated; faulty reconnaissance had informed them a large army was on its way, and their commanders feared they would be out numbered. It was too late for Mustafa. During the exchange of fire he was struck in the head and died hours later in the field hospital. In the annals of republican history, the small skirmish became a great victory, and Mustafa Pasha was proclaimed a Nationalist hero. In a park near the government buildings of present-day Ankara stands a statue commemorating his heroism. He who cared little for honors would have been bemused.

I was numb, but I could not grieve; he was where he wished to be. Mustafa courted death to redress the balance. He was a wounded man. The wounds were psychic, invisible — every day a punishment for surviving his beloved son. In the days and weeks that followed, time tumbled past. There was none of the relentlessness I had lived through after Burnham's death. We were busy, Florence and I, preoccupied with the business of relieving suffering. There was no time for grief. At night, as I fell into bed worn by work, Mustafa's voice returned neither to comfort nor assure me but to remind me this is where we are all going, this is all we have—the moment, nothing more. Ah, Mustafa, I think of you often, although the sound of your voice has faded and I no longer see your face in my dreams.

Meanwhile Annie, slowed by illness, began to vanish in front of our eyes. She knew she was dying, but the specter of death made her work twice as hard. We could not stop her. As the Greek invasion and civil war encroached on Angora we moved between cities, back and forth from Konya to Kayseri and Sivas, keeping Admiral Bristol up to date with conditions in the Nationalist zone. I like to think of myself as an impartial observer rather than an amateur spy, although my drawing skills gave more information than many written reports. When Annie died in the harsh winter of 1922 Florence and I wept for our loss; no matter how familiar we had become with dying, the finality of death was always a shock. We continued her work and became known to Christian and Muslim Anatolians alike as colleagues of Annie Allen, and no one questioned what we were doing there.

On October 1, 1922, the Grand National Assembly voted to separate the Caliphate and Sultanate; then the Sultanate was abolished in a direct challenge to the legitimacy of the government in Istanbul. Consequently it was Ismet Inonu, not the sultan, who represented Turkey at the signing of the Lausanne Treaty, where the borders of modern Turkey were defined despite vehement opposition of the Allies. Colonial aspirations were defeated, the nationalists prevailed, and Ismet returned home a hero. In fall 1923 the last foreign troops left Istanbul, a year after Sultan Mehmet IV and his household had been smuggled out of the palace in a British army ambulance. They were placed on a ship to Malta, never to return. His cousin Abdulmecit was named caliph, but not for long.

When the Caliphate was finally dismantled, the imperial household was disbanded and the last traces of the Ottoman world erased. Halide was saddened when she heard tales of elderly palace ladies who suddenly found themselves destitute and alone after knowing no other home except the imperial harem. The Ottoman court at Yildiz had been part of her childhood, and she retained an ambivalent affection for some of the more arcane institutions.

After the Declaration of the Republic in 1923, Mustafa Kemal became president while still officially commander of the army. General Ismet was named prime minister, inextricably linking government and the armed forces. Kemal's vision for modern Turkey did not end there. In the space of two years, a civil code was adopted to replace the old sharia-based legal system. The fez was banned, women were given equal rights, religious schools and courts were closed, dervish lodges and shrines were shuttered, and the institutions of Islam came under state control. Reform came at a price: dissenters were silenced and leaders either imprisoned or hung. I don't recall when Halide and Adnan first developed misgivings about the nature of Mustafa Kemal's rule. By the following year they had joined with other Nationalist colleagues to form a democratic opposition party, the Progressive Republicans.

Four close colleagues from the early days in Angora were hung for treason, accused of plotting the assassination of Mustafa Kemal. Traumatized by the summary brutality, Halide and Adnan lost faith in the new government. Tainted by association and hemmed in by suspicion, they made the difficult decision to go into exile, leaving the nascent republic for which they had sacrificed everything. They told no one save Halide's sister Nighar. When the news came out I happened to be living in a dilapidated studio near the American consulate; for a few months at least I had returned to painting, inspired by sketches made during my time in Anatolia. I was shocked, as if hearing of sudden death. Now they were all gone, my beloved Turkish friends.

Adnan and Halide settled first in Paris before moving to London, where they rented an apartment close to Hampstead Heath. Through smuggled letters I learned that the rural setting reminded Halide of the garden in Besiktas where she played as a child. Their flight ended that part of my life; my story is told. Now I can put down my pen, blot the last sentence, and stare idly at the leaves falling to the sidewalk. Light flashes across the window of the brownstone across the street. The day is drawing to a close.

# Reader's Discussion Group Questions

# Discussion Questions

1. When Mary arrives in Istanbul there is a sense that her grief for her husband, who was lost in the Great War, will never end. To what extent is the passion she feels for her fallen husband assuaged by her visit to his grave in Normandy? What are the other stages of her grief? To what extent does getting lost in an alien world relate to severing her ties with her old life? Have you ever traveled to escape a terrible personal loss? To what degree does entering another world help fill up a void at your core?

2. When Connie refuses to get out of the car to tour the mosque with Mary, what does her reluctance to mingle in Turkish life say about her as a person? Does the spouse of a diplomat have a responsibility to understand the culture she or he is posted to?

3. Mary comes to Istanbul to visit her sister. Or does she? How well do the sisters understand each other? Does their mutual understanding grow during Mary's visit?

4. When Connie returns to the States to have her child, what impression will she give her friends and relatives about Istanbul? Will these impressions say more about Istanbul or about Connie?

5. Did you find Middle East events of the 21st century coloring your impressions while you read the book?

6. In 1919, Britain had for a long time been the world's superpower. In what ways does the Britain of the novel resemble the United States of today?

7. The United States is often criticized for barging into Middle East affairs without any deep understanding of the people or any enduring native stake in the outcome. In what sense might Mary be described the same way? She was an American without any claim to Turkish ancestry; she has no background in Turkish affairs; and yet there she is on the front lines dining with the generals and writing their press releases.

8. Turkey and its affairs and influence occupy the front pages of today's world newspapers. How much attention did Turkey receive from the rest of the world at the time of Kazan's novel?

9. At what point, if any, did you realize that many of Kazan's characters are historical figures? Admiral Bristol was an American naval commander, and he and Robert Dunn were both intelligence officers. Florence Billings and Annie Allen were well-known social activists. Halide was an important literary person. Her husband, Dr. Adnan Adivar, was a prominent politician. And Mustafa's destiny was the future of the country. How did their historical realities contribute to your experience of the fiction Kazan creates?

10. President Woodrow Wilson saw the need for a League of Nations decades before the founding of the United Nations. He also demanded "self-determination" for the defeated Ottoman territories. If he hadn't suffered a stroke, how would the history of Turkey and the region be different? How is that tension expressed in the novel?

11. Do you think the Allied refusal to intervene during the Greek invasion of Smyrna has any parallels to our present day Middle East—particularly Libya and Syria?

12. In what ways does Mary's encounter with the boy fleeing the British soldiers change the trajectory of her life? Is this an example of Fate, or Will, or simple Coincidence?

13. Why doesn't Mary tell Connie about the papers in her possession? What are the competing forces for her loyalty? Does she do the right thing? What would you have done with your own sibling in that situation?

14. What are the similarities and differences between the protest in Sultanahmet Square and the mass protests in Tahrir Square that gave rise to the Arab Spring in Cairo?

15. After visiting Latife Hanim and passing her childhood home, Halide laments that the old Ottoman way of life is dying. How does the novel reflect these changes? What does the story tell us about day-to-day Ottoman life?

16. Were you surprised when Mary went to stay with Halide? Had she reached the point where she could never return to her old life? Or were there other points at which you thought Mary might still have returned to the safety and predictability of the American Embassy?

17. After indignantly denying there were any arms in the soup kitchen, Halide shows Mary the hidden arms cache. Were you surprised? Does Halide tell her in order to emphasize Mary's complicity in forthcoming violence? Or is it a sign of her trust in Mary? Or both?

18. What do you think of Connie's insistence on having her child in America? During 1919 hundreds of children were born every day in Turkey. Was Connie right to insist on returning to New York? What would you have done? Remember that in 1919 New York was a rugged six-week ocean voyage from Istanbul. On the other hand, malaria was a very real threat in Turkey. If your daughter were in Istanbul today, would you wish her to return to the States to have her first child?

19. Sergeant Parks is as close as we get to a villain in the novel. But is the source of his threat understandable? Is he simply a bad man—was he, do you suppose, filled with the same vengeance and bitterness before the death of his brother? Was he always a dangerous character? Suffering from her own traumatic grief, does Mary ironically have a bond with the man who wishes her destruction? Are there Sergeant Parks types in British and American uniforms today?

20. Both Halide and Mustafa had traditional Ottoman fathers who nonetheless gave their children a Western education. What does this tell you about their culture? Are Halide and Mustafa more worldly than the Americans in the story?

21. How does Mary's work as a painter evolve? How does it reflect her geographical journey? Her emotional journey?

22. As a young woman Mary fell under the spell of her brilliant husband, Burnham. Soon after her arrival in Istanbul, she appears to fall under the spell of the charismatic Halide. She then falls under the powerful spell of Mustafa Pasha. At the end of the novel, whose spell is Mary under?

23. Halide describes their journey to Angora as a "Nationalist Hadj." Why does she make this comparison? Do you agree with it?

24. When Mustafa Kemal thanks Mary for her courage in rescuing the documents from Halil, she deflects the praise, as she does throughout the novel. Is she simply being modest, or was she demonstrating true courage? What might you have done in the same situation?

25. Mustafa tells Mary that life is fleeting and urges "Let us take what we can." He is neither the first nor the last man to press this line of argument in pursuit of a woman. Do you agree with his assessment of their predicament?

26. Mary suffers from a crippling fever during her train journey. Is the fever merely a physical malady, or are there emotional and psychological aspects to it?

27. Do you think Mustafa ever believed there was a real romantic future for the two of them? Did Mary know all along that long-term togetherness with Mustafa was impossible? Were Mary and Mustafa and the love that entwined them doomed from the start?

28. To what extent is Mary a passive hero being thrust into the flow of history and to what extent does she assert her own will upon events?

29. Even as she serves Halide's cause, Mary is expected to report to the admiral. The admiral is expected to be a loyal ally to the British, yet he shields Mary from their jurisdiction. We often demand total loyalty from those close to us. But is it always possible?

30. Did you expect some romantic development between Mary and Admiral Bristol? How does the author introduce that prospect? How would

Mary's story have changed if she and the Admiral had commenced a deeper relationship?

31. When Mary asks Halide how she reconciles her faith with her nationalist beliefs, her response credible?

32. Annie Allen and Florence Billings were real women who devoted their lives to Near East Relief, a missionary organization funded by Americans. They built schools, orphanages and hospitals. Is, as some believe, missionary work a form of colonialism?

33. Is Mary's response to the news of Mustafa's death understandable? How does this reaction differ from her reaction to the news of her husband's death at the book's outset?